monsoonbooks

YOU MIGHT WANT TO MARRY MY HUSBAND

Yap Swi Neo was born and raised in Malacca, Malaysia, and now lives in Singapore. She is a retired educator with over 40 years of teaching in schools in Malaysia, and in institutes of higher learning in Singapore. Swi enjoys recapturing her youth in stories that bring to life old Malaysia and Singapore and the struggles of women in society, stories to be enjoyed by young and old alike. Swi is the author of two published short stories and co-author of six books on the teaching of English.

T0168833

You Might Want To Marry My Husband

Yap Swi Neo

monsoon

monsoonbooks

First published in 2021
by Monsoon Books Ltd
www.monsoonbooks.co.uk

No.1 The Lodge, Burrough Court, Burrough on the Hill,
Leicestershire LE14 2QS, UK.

ISBN (paperback): 9781912049981
ISBN (ebook): 9781912049998

Cover design by Cover Kitchen.

'Is The Soup Done?' first published in *My Life, My Stories* (Verena Tay, ed.) Singapore: National Library Board, Singapore (2015); 'In Towkey Lee's Mansion' first published in *The Best Asian Short Stories 2020* (Zafar Anjum, ed.) Singapore: Kitaab (2020).

A Cataloguing-in-Publication data record is available from the British Library.

Printed and bound in Great Britain by Clays Ltd, Elcograf S.p.A.
23 22 21   1 2 3

Contents

Is The Soup Done?

I grew up in a Peranakan family. The Peranakans are
descendants of early Chinese male settlers in Malaysia,
who worked in tin mines, rubber estates and as labourers
in the towns. They married local Malay women and over
time evolved their own sub-culture, a blend of Chinese
and Malay customs, evident in their food and patois. The
centre of the household was the dapur, *the kitchen. The*
matriarch ruled the dapur *and all daughters were taught*
the fine art of Peranakan culinary arts. We spoke our own
patois known as Baba Malay, as well as English, Malay
and Chinese.

When I think of Tua-Ee, my first aunt, I always see her in her
samfoo[1], bent over the wood fire, carefully stirring her soups over
the red mama stove in Grandfather's house. She was the queen of
soups, and her queen of queen soups was her salted vegetable and
duck soup.

'Watch. Duck, one duck – cut into six pieces. Two ducks, how
many pieces? You know why we cut one duck into six pieces?
Why?' That was a rhetorical question. We were asked thousands

---

1 A blouse resembling a cheongsam cropped to the hips, and a
matching pair of trousers.

of times, 'Why?'

'Because we boil the soup s-l-o-w-l-y for a very long time. Why?' Another rhetorical question.

'See?' Yes, we saw.

'Now we pour two tablespoons of brandy and rub into the duck. Why? To season the duck. Brandy, *wangi sekali*[2], gives it a very nice rich flavour. Leave it aside. Now we prepare *kiam chye*[3]. One duck, one kati[4] *kiam chye,* so two ducks, how many katis? Cut into quite large pieces, wash in plenty of water, then soak for about thirty minutes. Why?' In Tua-Ee's kitchen, there were always many 'why' questions to answer.

Our kitchen was about four metres from the main house. It was a four-pillar structure about two-and-a-half by five-and-a-half-metres in size. It was an open-kitchen concept, decades ahead of its time. Three sides had plank 'walls' about thirty centimetres from the cement floor and about one metre high. Between the top of the walls and the roof was a one-metre ventilation space for the smoke to ease itself out like the genie from the lamp. The walls were painted an oil-based black paint, to prevent wood rot. The roof was made of attap, thatched leaves made from the nipa palm.

On the right side of the kitchen wall was a zinc door opening to the outdoor wash area, with a tap and a *kolam*, a cemented one-metre-high water container. We washed our cutlery and utensils with Sunlight soap. A bar of amber-coloured Sunlight soap was twenty centimetres long. It was an opaque and pretty bar.

---

2 Malay for 'very aromatic'.
3 Pickled salted mustard leaves.
4 The standard measurement then was kati and taels. 16 taels make one kati. One kati is approximately 0.5 kilograms.

When held against the light, the soft threads of amber permeated through the Sunlight. It was cut into three: a piece for the kitchen, a piece for the bathroom and a piece beside the well to bathe the six dogs we had. Alongside the outer walls were nails on which we hung our pots and pans and washbasins. There was a place for everything and everything had its place.

The kitchen still stands in retired silent majesty, having provided comfort for the bellies of the family over three generations. Generations of migrant lizards and geckos, the true 'children of the soil', have enjoyed all the privileges of citizenship in the kitchen. We never knew where these *cicaks* came from but, having arrived, they made the kitchen their domain in perpetuity. They could never be driven out of their homeland, relocated or even teased away. Their singing, gossiping and complaining broke the silence of the night, but these squatters never frightened any of us. Time and again, when they were too noisy, we playfully tried to smoke them out, never very successfully. They played hard to get, darting and leaping across the attap. When threatened, they shot their little tails off. The little wriggling tail, wherever it was, was fascinating to watch, until the wriggling ceased. Not to worry, lizards will never be without a tail – lose one, grow another one. Cicaks and geckos have feelings too. They showed their displeasure with tiny little droppings during the night. Eventually death would come; we swept away their dearly departed. At other times they celebrated new life, leaving us empty little white shells on the stove tops as 'News Flash – Latest Addition' signs. Sometimes I wondered whether we had unknowingly cooked a lizard alive in our stoves. My cousin assured me we had not;

neither cicaks nor geckos had fallen off their homes into any of Tua-Ee's soups.

Looking into the kitchen from the house, we saw the red inverted-U cement block, solidly staid. Into it was carved papa stove, mama stove and baby stove, which took up three-quarters of the surface. The other quarter was the utility space for the cooking oil, various sauces and other condiments. Below the stoves was the storage space for the firewood. Each stove had a different purpose. Papa stove was for the big woks and pots, which played their part during celebrations and festivals. The papa-stove pot could easily hold four ducks for the salted vegetable and duck soup. Mama stove was for the smaller pots and woks for daily use. Baby stove was for the kettle and pots to boil eggs and heat up leftovers.

The morning of the last Sunday of the month was the morning of the middle-aged Malay 'firewood man'. The affable *pakcik*[5], with a light whip on his bullock, parked his cart right beside the kitchen. Pakcik, always smiling, had rubber tree logs chopped into two-foot-long pieces, and split into five to six pieces. He patiently unloaded the wood at the designated area beside the kitchen. After a cup of coffee and two slices of toast, he waved us goodbye with, '*Satu bulan lagi, saya datang.*' True to his word, he would come by the following month.

Tua-Ee taught us how to dry the pieces of firewood thoroughly, to arrange them in their storage place under the stove, to light a fire and, very importantly, how to douse the fire after the kitchen work was done. Her instructions were clear and precise: 'Arrange

---

5 Malay for 'uncle'; also a term of address.

four thicker pieces parallel. Then arrange the other pieces crisscrossed up to waist high. Why? This is to allow air to flow between the pieces of wood and dry them more efficiently.' When fully dried, we stacked the pieces of wood in neat piles under the stoves. Everything was within reach, ready for the preparation of our meals.

However, during the rainy season, the pieces of wood became damp. Just damp, not wet. Tiny white-grey fungi slowly pushed their sleepy heads through little eye slits in the wood, and then were in a hurry to mature into adulthood, ready for the taking. Their seemingly incessant screams, 'Eat me! Eat me!' like the 'EAT ME' cake that Alice found in her wonderland, before they grew into such a tremendous size, were deafening. We silenced them. Well, they wanted to get into hot soup, so we obliged! A soup of fried garlic and chicken stock was allowed to boil, 'Eat me!' added, two beaten eggs poured in, chopped green onions and parsley thrown in, a tornado stir given. After it had passed the 'Is the soup done?' test, it was deliciously slurped down. It was our soup, not a soup for anyone outside our family circle. That was more than half a century ago.

On weekends and holidays, our favourite breakfast was hot toast. After the morning coffee was brewed on baby stove, the cinders of the wood made a perfect toaster. Slices of bread were placed on double wire mesh and beautifully toasted to perfection. They were then turned over, and Planta margarine spread on them, topped with a sprinkling of sugar or sometimes condensed milk. We watched our toast with unblinking Barbie doll eyes, as the sugar melted on the margarine, emitting the most delicious aroma.

Tua-Ee, though petite, ruled in the kitchen like an Amazon matriarch, dignified, strong and completely in charge. To her, the kitchen demanded respect. 'The *dapur*[6] is the source of life. Life needs food. No kitchen, no food!' Every day we would help her with chores such as preparing shallots. (Shallots sliced into cross sections, lengthwise, pounded, smashed, or left whole, gave different flavours and were to be used in different dishes.) Working mostly from the square kitchen table in the middle of the kitchen, Tua-Ee would share and discuss news, dispense judgements and point out lessons for us children: 'See what happened when that Lucy ... always ... People say he got ... So, remember ... You must always do ... Don't ...'

There were more don'ts than dos. Tua-Ee was very emphatic that we remember whatever she had taught (be it recipes or life skills) and made us repeat instructions after her so often that her 'Remember!' is still remembered to this day.

The day's lessons were usually taught in just the right amount of time for Tua-Ee's soups to be made and tasted. For instance, her salted vegetable and duck soup simmered gently over papa stove for several hours. When the twelve pieces of dried tamarind, two-inch piece of ginger, slightly bashed, and twelve salted sour plums had obediently taken their places in the six-litre soup pot, Tua-Ee, left hand on hip, right hand holding a ladle of boiling soup, would taste the soup. Then she would administer the test. Looking straight into our eyes, she would ask, 'Is the soup done?' We had to answer, yes or no, for with Tua-Ee, one was wise not to

---

6 Malay for 'kitchen'.

complain, only comply. When we got it right, she teased, 'So c-l-e-v-e-r to guess.' If we got it wrong she lamented, 'Next time, what would your mother-in-law say, ah? Your mother n-e-v-e-r teach you. Where to put your face? So *malu*!' My cousin (her daughter) and I, the fifteen-year-old and the eleven-year-old, swore we would never ever get married and live with mothers-in-law who would administer the 'Is the soup done?' examination and put our mothers to shame.

'Tua-Ee, how will we know when the soup is done?'

'You will know, you will know.'

Even with Tua-Ee's teaching, I have never known whether my soups are done. Today the instructions on the slow cooker, thermos cooker and pressure cooker decide.

To Tua-Ee, family recipes were not only taught; to ensure that the girls in the family learnt, she instructed, 'Copy the recipe. You young people nowadays are not interested in cooking. *Dulu kala*[7], in the time of my grandmother, at five years old I was peeling onions and frying eggs and pounding sambal. Copy the recipe, or you will forget!' We dutifully wrote in our '555' exercise book, our very first recipe, *sambal belacan*, a shrimp paste and chilli condiment, the must-have condiment at every meal.

Tua-Ee dictated, 'Sambal belacan. Cut out a one-finger thick piece *belacan*[8], eight red chillies, three pieces *daun limau perut*[9]. For a very spicy sambal, don't deseed the chillies. Cut the spine off the kaffir lime leaf. Grill the belacan slowly over the cinders till you smell the cooked aroma. How to pound. Make sure the

7 Malay for 'in the olden days'.
8 Shrimp paste.
9 Kaffir lime leaf – an aromatic herb.

mortar is dry. Pound the belacan and chillies, not too fine, then add limau perut. Continue pounding till the leaves are very fine. *Sedap sekali*, very delicious, yah?'

The person who *tumbok-ed* the sambal got a special treat – the *nasi tumbok*. After the sambal has been scooped into a serving bowl, half a bowl of freshly cooked rice was lightly pounded in the *lesong*, or mortar, to absorb the sambal residue. With a squeeze of calamansi juice, the nasi tumbok was eaten off the mortar using one's fingers. My cousin and I licked our fingers often with such gusto that Tua-Ee cheekily teased, 'Next time your mother-in-law will say: you ah, *ta' seronoh*, so *sedap*, until *jilat jari!*[10] This not KFC, lick your fingers 'cos it's so delicious. So un-daughter-in-law behaviour!' All this happened more than five decades ago. It never occurred to Tua-Ee that we might marry 'others', and there would not be a need to *tumbok* sambal belacan. For instance, today's sambal belacan recipe tells us:

Tools required:
- A mini blender or food processor.
- A non-stick pan to toast the belacan.

Tips:
1. When de-seeding chilli, wear disposable plastic gloves to prevent chilli burn.
2. Belacan has a pungent aroma. Open your kitchen windows when toasting belacan.

---

10 'You ah, such unladylike behaviour, so delicious that you lick your fingers!' ['Ta' seronoh' is Baba Malay for 'improper' or 'inappropriate' ('unladylike' in this context); from the Malay 'tidak senonoh' ('not appropriate').]

3. Put away all laundry (if you have them in the kitchen) if you do not wish the belacan smell to permeate into your laundry.

4. Air your kitchen after cooking

5. Serve with calamansi. If you do not have calamansi, substitute with larger lime or lemon (try your best to buy calamansi as it gives the best taste).

I can hear Tua-Ee gasp for breath. '*Apa ini?* What's all this ah? You cannot use a blender to pound sambal! You cannot use lemon juice! Alamak! No mother would want you as daughters-in-law! If you marry, we would be put to shame by your mother-in-law, grandmothers-in-law, sisters-in-law, aunts-in-law and whoever else. *Malu sekali*, so shameful!'

I forget. Today's recipes are for city dwellers in housing estates where the kitchen, the laundry area and the pantry are a three-in-one. The sound of pounding mortar and pestle might annoy neighbours and we might be advised not to prepare sambal belacan at home, or if we still wanted to, we must check whether our neighbours are home and ask for their permission. Or we can simply buy a bottle of factory-prepared sambal belacan from NTUC supermarket! Cutting calamansi into two and washing lime leaves do not generate any noise, so that's allowed. I can 'see' the size of the piece of Tua-Ee's belacan, as they came in brick-size blocks then. Today, belacan comes in granules, blocks or balls, in different colours and textures. What then is the size of a piece of belacan?

Tua-Ee whispered, 'Look. Use your eyes.'

All of Tua-Ee's recipe ingredients and instructions in basic English and Malay had parentheses to explain and clarify further. My cousin and I and anyone reading them just cannot go wrong. When I set up my own home, I read my '555' exercise book with nostalgia, marvelling at how times had changed over one generation. Tua-Ee's views reflected her time. What did she get for her marketing? 25 cents onions for two recipes; 15 cents nice red chillies for three servings of sambal belacan; $1.50 *bak kut*[11] soup base enough for two servings. Her advice on choosing the freshest ingredients still resonates in me:

'When you buy prawns, always see the head; if loose from body, not fresh; also smell, if not good smell, then not fresh.' For added emphasis she made us write in parentheses: '(Don't buy)'.

'To buy chickens, choose noisy ones[12]. If they are not noisy it means they are not healthy, already *lemah*.'

'Brown-shell are better than white-shell eggs.'

'Brinjals, choose light ones, heavy ones are full of seeds.'

'Worms and bugs make their homes in dried beans, so look carefully that there are no holes in the beans.'

She had her favourite stalls and gave explicit instructions on whom to buy from. Buy from Hong Huat. Buy from Ah Pek, don't buy from the son. If Ah Pek not there, don't buy.'

When the salted vegetable and duck soup had passed the 'Is the soup done' test, Tua-Ee instructed, 'Leave the lid on. The soup will continue to boil. Just now so much water. Now, see, less soup already.' Before dinner, the soup was gently reheated and

11 Herbal pork bone soup.
12 Markets sold live chickens. We chose our chicken and had it
    slaughtered and dressed.

just before serving, two tomatoes, quartered, were tossed in. Like Oliver Twist, we watched as our soup bowls were filled with a piece of duck, several pieces of salted vegetables, and a wedge of very red tomato and piping hot soup. There was enough, we need not ask for more. Together with a serving of sambal belacan and half a calamansi, a plate of freshly boiled rice, we feasted. There was never a need for words.

Now, two generations later, my cousin and I, two grandmothers, can only sit side by side, in silence, but knowing exactly that we still hear Tua-Ee testing us, 'Is the soup done?' Tua-Ee's pencil-written recipes in her yellowed, oiled, torn '555' exercise books are barely legible. The last written recipe dated 17/8/79 was 'Thousand Island Dressing'. We never knew whether she had prepared that. Our own '555' exercise books with pencil-written recipes have long been replaced with published coloured recipe books such as *The Best of Balti Cooking, Thai Made Easy* and *No Mess Baking*. Our kitchen houses Teflon utensils, the slow cooker, the thermos pot, the microwave oven together with blenders and choppers and electronic knife sharpeners.

No, we do not miss papa stove, mama stove, baby stove, the cicaks and geckos. But Tua-Ee, we miss you; we miss your salted vegetable and duck soup. It is the best in the world. We are glad you have taught us well. We love you.

First published in *My Life, My Stories* (Verena Tay, ed.) Singapore: National Library Board, Singapore (2015)

My Sisters, My Teachers

I was educated in Convent of the Holy Infant Jesus (CHIJ), usually referred to as French Convent, as the first girls schools were set up by French missionaries. The Sisters were from France, England, Ireland and several were local Chinese and Indians. We wondered whether Sisters found their attire – their layers of petticoats, headdress, and socks and shoes – a 'heater'. Despite their strict discipline, we loved our Sisters. We are what we are today because of our Sisters.

Walking into primary school, Convent of the Holy Infant Jesus (CHIJ), Bandar Hilir Road, Malacca[13], we could never escape the prowling, stalking eyes of the Sisters. There were Sisters here, there, everywhere – at the school gate, classrooms, office, bookshop, canteen, chapel, playground. We could never escape their binocular vision and binaural steréo hearing; the Caucasian faces and hands peeping out of the ankle-length black tunic covered by a scapular, which was an apron that went over the shoulders and covered the front and back of the tunic; a coif covered the head completely; socks and shoes; and often their

---

13 One of the thirteen states in Malaysia, 'Melaka' in Malay.

metre-long rosary swinging round their necks as they walked very fast chasing us. We wondered then whether the Sisters had ears and hair, both of which we never saw.

Facing the main gate of the school was the grotto of Our Lady of Fatima, the Mother of Christ. She was serene and beautiful in her long white robes, her hands holding a Rosary in prayer, and a crown on her head. Often we spent a minute asking her to intercede for us, for whatever. The primary school was a three-sided double-storey rectangular building. The school building was educational. We learnt about the Parlour, the Visitor's Parlour and the Morning Room leading to Reverend Mother Margaret Mary, the Principal's Office and beyond that the General Office. On the left was the Piety Shop, where we could buy rosaries, crucifixes, bibles and other Catholic paraphernalia. On the left longer side of the rectangle were the school hall and a row of classrooms. On the right side of the rectangle was the canteen. Beyond it was the orphanage. The orphans attended school with us. During recess the older girls helped out in the canteen. The fourth side of the rectangle, facing the Parlour, was the seawall and a barbwire ran across the top to prevent us from jumping into the sea, or to prevent undesirable guests jumping in. There was a short flight of concrete steps, enough for us to peer at what was in the sea – mainly household rubbish, as there was no proper garbage collection then. Sister Rita, Discipline Sister, warned us that should we fall over, there would be no 'Big Fish' to swallow us then spit us out to safety.

The upper floors of the building housed classrooms. Facing the playground was a large triangular balcony jutting between the joints of two blocks. The playground was the centrepiece, right in the middle of the school, like the city square. Down the middle of the playground, a pathway led from the entrance to the gazebo two metres from the seawall. Six gigantic, majestic *angsana* trees lined the driveway on the right. Running alongside the right of the angsanas was a low hibiscus hedge, brilliantly coloured blooms of red, orange, white, pink, formed a colourful curtain going into the Canteen, which doubled up as a Sports Hall. While the angsana provided perfect shade for us to play our games in, the hibiscus hedge taught us life skills such as how to catch camouflaged match-head green spiders that we kept in little bottles. Often the tiny ones died, and Sister Rita rained fire and fury on us. Occasionally, tiny birds set up nests, and we were like little mothers eyeing the eggs. Sister Rita reminded us not to pick or touch the delicate eggs as we might break the brittle shells; we were not to pat the fledglings because mummy bird might reject the little chirpy ones. Maybe we could send the little birds to the orphanage.

The Convent Sisters educated us in many things, one of which was encouraging us to run. 'Girls, you must learn to run very, very fast. Go ahead, run some more!' The Sisters were emphatic in their words, always repeating them.

Later in upper primary we were taught the reason and value of being able to run very, very fast. Sister told us, 'You must be able to run very, very fast. If boys chase you, you can run away very, very fast. Don't let any boy catch you. Boys catch you, they do very, very bad things to you.'

We wondered aloud, then, why would boys want to catch

girls? What were the bad things they would do to us girls! Maybe like our brothers, they would pinch us or cut our hair or steal our homework! It was scary. So we all ran very, very fast every day in the school playground. That explained how secondary CHIJ girls earned our school many trophies for many years, running the 100 yards[14], the 220 yards, the 4 x 100 relays, and of course the hurdles at the Annual Inter-School Meet.

We were comfortable because the angsana trees fanned us as we ran about. Back in class, sweaty and panting, the Sister would ask, 'So girls, did you play? And run?' and she was pleased. When we told her we were sweaty, her response was, 'Girls, girls, girls, horses sweat; people perspire. You are not horses.' And later Sisters taught us, 'Goats have kids, people have children.'

Once every two years the Reverend Mother Superior of the Infant Jesus Order in France visited her Sisters in the Federation of Malaya[15] and Singapore. The Sisters and teachers excitedly prepared us girls for her biennial visit to all her Convent schools and Sisters and of course the teachers and students. Instead of the daily twenty-minute Catechism class in the morning, we were taught a few French phrases: 'bonjour révérende mère supérieure', good morning Reverend Mother Superior; 'merci beaucoup', thank you very much (for visiting us); 'bienvenue dans notre école', welcome to our school; 'oui', yes; 'bonne journée', have a good day; 'nous sommes heureux de vous voir', we are happy to see you; 'revenir bientôt', come again soon; 'oui, Jésus nous

---

14 1 yard = 91.44 centimetres. Malaysia changed from imperial to
   metric units in 1972.
15 It was only on 16 September 1963 that Malaya and Singapore
   merged to became Malaysia.

aime', yes, Jesus loves us; *'avoir un bon voyage de retour'*, have a safe journey home. We were excited and learnt the phrases as instructed as we walked along the corridor, to class, to the canteen and to the toilet, and tested one another. For a few weeks we felt 'French' – sophisticated and cultured. I must confess I have forgotten all the French and used Google for the translations.

On that great day, Mother Superior, Reverend Mother and all the Sisters stood on the balcony on the second floor of the school. We lined up at the playground by class with our class teachers and looked up at Reverend Mother Superior while she looked down on us. We had not learnt the concepts of 'looking up' and 'looking down'. We were to dress in fresh uniform, clean white socks and shoes. As a special treat, all girls were to tie a white ribbon in their hair, regardless of length or style. I had short hair, so mother tied the white ribbon into a bow and clipped it on my hair. I thought we looked nice. On cue, hundreds of CHIJ girls gathered together to welcome Reverend Mother Superior, recited in unison as rehearsed, *'bonjour révérende mère supérieure'*, *'bienvenue dans notre école'*, *'nous sommes heureux de vous voir'*. Mother Superior gave a short speech, which we pretended to understand. On cue, when Reverend Mother clapped her hands, so did we. And then, *'oui, Jésus nous aime'*, *'revenir bientôt'*; *'avoir un bon voyage de retour'*. On that special day, every two years, we were treated to a stick of *'ice-cream potong'* of our choice – the red bean *kacang merah*, corn or coconut ice-cream popsicle. It was one great day and soon all the French was forgotten.

Primary school laid the foundations for a sound education. We were taught cursive handwriting in upper primary. The practice exercise books had wide straight lines and dashed lines between them. Each letter had a little 'tail' to join it to the next letter. We wrote our letters between the lower lines and the dashed lines, and the letters with a 'head' were to touch the upper straight lines.

We had poetry recitation lessons fortnightly. We learnt grammar and had to repeatedly write verb tenses in columns – Present Tense (Root Word), Past Tense, Past Perfect Tense. We copied short stories then created a similar one. We learnt spelling, and each mistake had to be corrected ten times.

We learnt Math – addition, subtraction, division and multiplication, fractions and story sums. We learnt to draw. Sister Henry gave us a picture to copy. For complicated pictures like a scenery, she drew one-inch grid lines. We did the same and got our drawings 'right'. In later lessons, we drew freehand. Sister told us a story and we drew a scene from the story. My most cherished story was Black Beauty. I drew Beauty many times. I had a copy of *Black Beauty*, wrote my name in it and dated it 7 July 1957.

Soon, primary school was over. At our last assembly as primary school girls, Reverend Mother reminded us we were no longer girls. We were young ladies and to behave as such. We felt so adult, and promised her we would behave as adults. It was a tearful farewell to our Sisters and non-Sisters teachers who had brought us from arranging the letters of the alphabet to create words and stories to composing limericks, educating us on the different purposes of Parlours, Annexes, Meeting Rooms and Morning Rooms, narrating the fascinating stories of Moses and miracles of Jesus.

We crossed Bandar Hilir Road to CHIJ Secondary School.

The design of CHIJ Secondary was much the same as the primary school. It was a U-shaped double-storey building. A large crucifix dominated the front stretch of the garden between the school fence and the school. A small gate on the left led to the bicycle shed. The main entrance, the base of the 'U' had the parlour in the middle where the teacher on duty stationed herself. She eyed us and we never knew what she was looking for. Classrooms stretched on both sides. From the parlour we walked to the rectangular hall, behind which was the canteen and beyond that the washrooms. On the right side of the hall was the school field and four badminton courts and a row of classrooms and the domestic lessons classrooms – two kitchens and a sewing room. As with the primary school across the road, all the upper floors were classrooms. However, there were no angsana trees to shade us, and no gazebo to sit in to giggle our secrets. Sisters repeatedly reminded us we were young ladies and to behave as such.

What was different academically? Sister Martha, my English teacher, made the lessons difficult as she explained that the more difficult the lesson, the more we learnt. We had to write compositions on given topics with no 'helping words'; comprehension passages were longer; vocabulary lists were more difficult. We concluded she had to live up to her name – Martha the Martyr-er! She immersed us in the beauty of the works of Shakespeare, Wordsworth and other poets. Eventually when we did well in our Literature and English, we paid tribute to Sister Martha. We had new subjects like Malay Language, History, General Science, Physical Education, Music, Art without grid lines and Scripture Studies. In Geography we used a length of thread to measure lengths of rivers.

Music lessons included singing 'Danny Boy', 'Home on the Range', 'Greensleeves', 'The Ash Grove' and 'Amazing Grace'. Irish Sister Monica taught us the Irish jig. We paid unwavering attention as she lifted her skirt and exposed her black buckled shoes and white socks and layers of petticoat as she twirled, kicked and jumped, yet we could not see her feet. We enjoyed the Saint Bernard's Waltz and barn dances. We were fully English educated.

Our fist Domestic Science lesson was to brew a cup of tea. Sister Alexis taught us the proper way to brew and serve tea. We were given a tea tray, on which was a teacup and saucer, a teaspoon, a teapot, a tea leaf strainer on a tea strainer saucer, a tea milk jug, a tea sugar bowl, tea leaves in a tin, a cloth napkin and a teapot cosy.

'To make tea, you need a tea tray. This is a teacup and saucer, and a teaspoon. Crockery for tea and coffee are different, don't mix them up. Put in a teaspoon of tea leaves for each cup and one for the pot. So if you're making tea for three persons, you would put in four teaspoons of tea leaves. Pour in a cup of boiling water for each cup and one for the pot. Then cover the pot with the tea cosy, for the leaves to seep and to keep the tea warm. Pour out the tea four-fifths full into the teacup, help yourself to the sugar and milk and stir gently and quietly, clockwise.'

Gently, quietly, clockwise were emphasized. That was how Sister Alexis introduced us into the polite English society of serving and drinking tea. We were amazed and fascinated. A teapot had a *baju* to wear, and such pretty ones in different patterns, colours and materials. When I told my mother we had been drinking tea all wrong, she snorted Sister '*kepala angin*', wind in the head.

Our next lesson was to prepare cucumber sandwiches to serve with tea. At thirteen years old, I was already pounding sambal belacan, boiling rice over a wood fire and frying eggs and vegetables but had never heard of cucumber sandwiches. We had bread and Planta margarine and a sprinkling of sugar, condensed milk or *kaya*[16] jam. We had learnt what would be served should we be invited to tea in polite English company. Sister Alexis must have drunk so much tea that she did look like a teapot.

It was in secondary school, when we were just a wee bit more aware of our sexuality, we decided that we wanted to be caught by the boys, though in primary school Sisters had instilled in us to learn to run very, very fast, so that boys would not be able to catch us and do bad things to us! How exciting! And what were those bad things boys could do to us? That was when our sex education began. French Sister Lucy with perfect skin and rosy cheeks, explained, 'If you sleep beside a boy, you will become pregnant! And you have no husband! And your parents will be so ashamed! And they will throw you out! And where will you go? You are a sinner. You will burn in hell!'

We believed our Sisters, our teachers. We did not want to shame our parents, be thrown out and burn in hell! We formed ourselves into our own vigilante corps. On bus rides, should one of us sit next to a boy and nod off, we were quick to pinch her hard, we did not want her to burn in hell.

Sister Rita, our primary school Discipline Teacher was our

---

16 Coconut jam.

Scripture lesson teacher. She taught us how to sleep the proper way. 'Kneel beside your bed, say thank you to Jesus for a good day and thank God, Jesus, and Mother Mary for keeping you safe, and you promise to be a good girl. Then lie on your back, fold your arms across your chest, close your eyes and go to sleep.'

'But Sister, why do we need to lie on our back and fold our arms?'

'Sister, I always sleep on my side,' some of us protested.

The good Sister explained, 'When Jesus sends his angels to visit you, you are ready to go with them.' That terrified us! The angels of death!

It was during a church camp that a priest answered the question: 'This is to ensure your hands are not where they shouldn't be.' Ha? Aren't our hands here on our sides? Where else could they be?

A few years after we completed school and were in higher education, the movie *To Sir With Love* was released. My classmates and schoolmates sang the theme song repeatedly. It described our emotions and sentiments for our school, our teachers and especially our beloved Sisters perfectly, especially this line:

But how do you thank someone who has taken you from crayons to perfume? It isn't easy, but I'll try

CHIJ Malacca, the first school for girls set up by the French Missionaries in the state, celebrated her 150th anniversary in October 2010, more than half a century after I left at sixteen. It was with great nostalgia that my classmates and I visited our school. The turnout of past pupils was a tremendous show of love for our Sisters and our Convent. The gala dinner at the largest hotel had tables along the corridors. We met past students in wheelchairs, with walkers, and walking sticks. My classmates present included those who flew in from Australia, Italy and the US. The cliché 'how time flies' was repeated hundreds of times. We were schoolmates and classmates, now we were grandmothers.

Today, no Sisters walked the convent corridors, no 360-degree compound eyes to watch over us, no unseen stereophonic ears to eavesdrop on our chatter, no quick tongues to advise us to run very, very fast, no noisy chatter of silly convent girls of old. The gazebo where we had imagined and giggled over many unmentionable thoughts was in such a state of disrepair it had to be torn down. The seawall that had protected us from falling over into the sea now looked into a mammoth commercial complex, a hospital of international repute, and a colossal housing estate looking into the Straits of Malacca. Of the six majestic angsana trees, five still stood a full twenty to thirty metres tall in glory with a full head of green foliage sweeping the blue skies. One, naked, yet regal in its nakedness, refused to be hewn down. Only these trees could tell the stories, the gossips, the tears, the joys of past convent girls who had played in their shade.

In Search Of The Perfect Jambu Batu Branch

This is a true account of my husband's brother's thoughts after my husband passed away. Their visits to Ah Kong and Ah Por were regular and cherished.

I don't know why I turned left, but I did. Perhaps it was driving into the sunrise; perhaps it was the silent whispers in the crisp stillness of dawn; perhaps I wanted to. It had been a long while since I turned left; too many years since Mummy passed away, since my grandparents passed away. Perhaps it was they who invited me to visit, perhaps I had wanted to but was too fearful to face ... face what I was not sure, perhaps driving into the sunrise evaporated the fear. So I drove into Segamat district[17] over the bridge into town. I couldn't remember the name of the river, Sungei something, a small river. Yes, the hospital was still there, the same hospital my grandparents, aunts and uncles were admitted to when sickness befell them. The same railway line on my left into Segamat Station, from where I had travelled many times to and from Kuala Lumpur, the city I was heading to. Squinting across that railway line, I got a glimpse of where I was born.

---

17 A district in south Malaysia.

* * *

'The train is coming!' yelled the children. The rumble and whistle of the long black machine could be heard kilometres into the town. The kids scrambled to wave to the passengers; whether their welcoming waves were reciprocated or even noticed did not matter.

'One day I am going to ride the train to Kuala Lumpur.'

'I want to be the train driver and blow the horn. Then Mama and Nai-Nai will know I'm in Segamat. I'll blow the horn three times for Nai-Nai, Mama and Papa.'

'I want to be the towkay[18] of the train, so I can go wherever I like, to America, Japan, Penang!'

* * *

The train had pulled into the station about three kilometres away. Other dreams had to be expressed with the next train.

Both sides of the road remained the same: single-storey houses, probably lived in by the next or even the next-next generation of Ah Kong[19]'s time. Their rather large properties boasted rich harvests of rambutan, durian, local cherries, stalks of sugar cane, mangoes, papayas, and many other fruit trees that I could no longer recognize. Then there it was, glaring at me accusingly, the jambu[20] tree. The jambu tree. How could I ever get the jambu tree out of my mind, out of my conscience?

---

18 Boss.
19 Grandfather – mother's father; Ah Por –mother's mother.
20 Local guava. There are many varieties, jambu batu is the seedy variety.

* * *

'Ah Sam, next time you come, no need bring chocolates, towels, food. We can buy here. You only bring jambu batu branch, nice straight ones. Bring ten, about my arm long good, but short little bit also can. Bring nice ones.'

'Sum-Ee, there are so many jambu trees. Behind Ah Kong's house there are two.'

'They not jambu batu. Only jambu. The floods take jambu batu trees. They take very long time to grow.'

'OK, promise. I bring 100!'

'Emkoi ni, emkoi ni, thank you.' The promise to third aunty – broken.

* * *

Further up nearer to town, on my right a row of double-storey shophouses of small businesses. Then there was an open area, in its natural state of firm red mud clay. There was the lone cinema, the only entertainment centre. The cinema where I had immersed myself in 'King Kong', pounding my chest with loud bellows to frighten everyone; or I was an orang minyak, naked and oiled in black oil, ransacking houses to find goodies till I was caught by the police; or I was an Emperor's warrior saving his kingdom from his enemies and I was a hero. But where was the cinema?

* * *

'Ah Kong watch movie, 'Pontianak[21] Kembali' showing. 40 cents only. Superman movie also showing. 40 cents only.'

* * *

Weekends were movie days. It did not matter what movie, a movie was a movie. Ah Kong and I watched Shaw Brothers Hong Kong productions, Cathay Keris' Malay movies and Hollywood movies.

Next to the cinema was another row of double-storey shophouses. Ah Kong's house was the first one. He and his family lived on the upper floor, and the first floor was his storeroom, where he stored the sacks of rice, sugar, flour, milk and other sundry goods for his sundry shop business about two kilometres up the road. The present owner had turned it into an office. At the back of Ah Kong's shophouse were two fine jambu batu trees.

* * *

That plea again. 'Ah Sam, next time you come, bring jambu batu branch, long like my arm, very straight. Emkoi ni, thank you.'

* * *

I yearned for second and third aunties, to tell them how sorry I was not to have kept my promise to get them the jambu batu branch, not that I couldn't find one, but that it was a lack of trying and not taking their pleas seriously.

---

21 Malay female ghost. The movie is *Return of the Pontianak.*

I was still not clear why I was left to stay with Ah Kong in Segamat. My two uncles and my elder brother had left to board in Saint Francis Institution, Malacca, so I was brought up and loved by my grandparents, Mummy's parents, as a son. I still remembered how often I had asked them if I should be a Pang instead. I stayed in the shophouse, where their love and attention to me overcame any discomfort of living in the working conditions of the sundry shop. It was my home.

* * *

'What are you doing Sum-Ee?' I asked every morning.

'Grinding hum-cha for lunch,' the same answer from Third Aunty. She was the hum-cha Queen.

The 'cha' was a paste of black tea leaves, peanuts, sesame seeds, fresh basil and coriander leaves. The oil from the nuts and seeds gave it a rich flavour, the herbs exude the aroma of the paste.

'Why use this stick to grind?'

'This not stick. This jambu batu branch, nice smell nice taste.'

* * *

The ingredients were ground in a hum-cha pot. The inner side was grooved, to help in grinding everything into a smooth paste. That was a Hakka pot, a pot to cherish. It was many years later I recognized the importance of hum-cha to our family. Sometimes Sum-Ee allowed me to help her grind. But the peanuts 'jumped out' of the pot, and I ate them. Ah Kong liked a strong mint, coriander and basil flavour. I didn't like the taste of mint very much. When Sum-Ee was not looking, I threw out half. But she had compound eyes all over her head, just like a fly's. I suspected she had eyes on her neck and shoulders too. She need not look at me to know what I was up to. This stick, this special stick, this jambu batu branch.

* * *

'The stick good, I hold grind cha. When you grow big you give Sum-Ee jambu batu branch, OK? Like this one good, very good.'

* * *

During the three years I lived with Ah Kong, aunty had ground down three jambu batu branches. The flecks off the jambu batu branch added flavour to the tea. It was also believed to have medicinal value.

In Grandfather's house, as in most Hakka homes, lunch was *hum-cha*, a much-loved Hakka meal. *Hum-cha* in Hakka means 'salty tea' and that is what it was. It was 'salty tea soup', served with rice and several finely chopped vegetable dishes fried with lots of garlic. When I was not grinding the tea, I was busy helping Nee-Ee, Second Aunty, in the kitchen, chopping the garlic and vegetables finely with my kiddy plastic knife. Three bowls of garlic to fry the ingredients for the *hum-cha* lunch. Several pieces of *taukwa*[22] were cut into small cubes, to be fried with finely sliced leeks; there were long beans, finely chopped pickled radish, and pounded dried prawns. And the topping was rice puffs.

---

22 Firm beancurd cakes.

Hum-cha is now a popular meal in food courts. But it can never be the same as that made by Nee-Ee and Sum-Ee. The commercial hum-cha was colourfully advertised Thunder Tea for whatever reason I could never understand. The *cha* was not the *hum-cha, cha* as I knew it. The meal was served with additional choices of chicken wings, omelette, sausages and whatever else the stall keepers chose to offer. What a shame that within two generations, our Hakka food culture has changed into something else.

* * *

'Lunch ready. Lai, cher. Cha very hot!' Nee-Ee called out.

* * *

We ate with Grandfather's five employees. We had a rice bowl, a pair of chopsticks and a Chinese spoon. Nee-Ee poured the boiling water into the *hum-cha* pot and stirred the soup with the jambu batu branch.

* * *

Ah Kong always sat me beside him. 'Ah Sam, cher, eat.' He scooped the first layer of rice into my bowl. 'Ah Sam, this taukwa and leeks, very good for you, long beans green vegetable, good for you, chaipoh[23] slightly salty, good taste, peanuts in the soup rich flavour. How cher, very good to eat. Careful Ah Sam, Nee-Ee scoop hot hum-cha for you. Now take rice puffs, see rice puffs float on soup? Rice we eat we live, so boiled rice at bottom of

---

23 Dried salted radish.

bowl our stomach always full. Rice puffs float, this means we stay up always.' We ate heartily and drank the *'cha'* off the bowl.

* * *

I stopped to eye Ah Kong's and my shophouse home, long past. I saw Ah Por's ducks scampering around the back lanes. Grandmother had reared some ducks, as there were plenty of spilled grains from the sacks of rice to feed them. Her special Hakka-style duck was duck stewed with fermented red tofu. She slaughtered the ducks and refused to let me watch, claiming that small children would suffer a pain in the neck forever. At four years old I believed her.

Ah Por prepared a large wok, poured in two tablespoons of oil, added a bulb of smashed unpeeled garlic, three to four pieces of fermented red tofu and mashed them into the oil, coated the duck with the marinade, added enough water to cover the duck, added dark sweet sauce and simmered it over a low charcoal fire until the duck was tender, about two hours. It was a duck dish no three-Michelin-star chef could compete with. When I was an adult working in Singapore, Ah Por still prepared it for me when I went home to her and Ah Kong. There were two additional ducks prepared for me to take home, one for me and one for my brother Pin. Ah Kong and Ah Por loved us both in the only way they knew how – completely, selflessly, unconditionally.

I crossed Segamat River. The river that had caused such great sorrows to so many businesses too many times. The river looked wide and deep, but the water, not given enough width and depth in the river, was revengeful and having consumed the banks was still hungry and went on to rampage the town. Something could have been done to widen and deepen the river to engage and overcome the waters, but nothing was done.

At the end of the bridge, on the only main road, was another row of shophouses. Ah Kong's sundry shop was third from the end of the row. He had a small office he shared with his bookkeeper. The shop was stacked to the ceiling with his stock. Extra stock was kept upstairs, where he slept. The present owner had turned the shop into a Chinese medicinal shop.

* * *

'*Ah Kong I want to sleep with you tonight.*'

'*No, you sleep at home, on your bed.*'

'*Ah Kong, people say upstairs you keep python to eat rats. Rats eat your rice.*'

'*Who say? Python eat me and you no more, Ah Kong! Don't believe story!*'

I still did not know whether Ah Kong had kept a python there.

'*Ah Sam, eat your breakfast. You will be late for school.*'

* * *

That was my very own Ah Por. She walked me to play school every morning and fetched me home. Ah Kong lunched with me and the workers, on Nee-Ee and Sum-Ee's freshly brewed *hum-cha*. After lunch, Ah Kong held my hand and we took a short walk to the fruit shop in the back lane and shared a *li*, a Chinese pear with me. We ate in silence in a world of our own. There was nothing more we needed to say. I was his son, he was my father. What I cherished most living with Ah Kong and Ah Por was their love and attention to me, a love I had never felt before. The shop with sacks of rice, sugar, milk, cooking oil, various sauces and biscuits was my home.

The big floods came unannounced. The river had swollen past the red 'DANGER' sign marker. It scooped up everything that stood in its way. Everyone was in fear, the fear increasingly darkened like the clouds. Before sacks of rice could be carried up to higher ground, the clouds burst open releasing another of its load. It appeared then that not every cloud had a silver lining. It frightened me to see our whole town half submerged in violent, gushing water, carrying with it Ah Kong's tins of Dutch Baby milk powder, sacks of sugar and flour twisting in a frenzy and leaving a trail of white as the flour dissolved, and the shards of dozens of bottles of sauces, together with other residents' chairs, rubbish, some animals, all fighting for breath and space in the watery beast. In a few short weeks, it would be our gentle friend again, and children would be happily fishing for *fighting fish*.

Ah Por wanted to save her ducks for her special red fermented bean paste duck stew. She suffered a nasty cut and gangrene set in. In her usual 'don't inconvenience anyone' philosophy she did not tell anyone; everyone was busy salvaging what they could, cleaning the mess and debris. The gangrene had spread. We brought her to Singapore General Hospital and, as she was a severe diabetic patient, her leg had to be amputated. She was never the same again, her movements were restricted, her fuss over her grandchildren tapered. The matriarch she was, her presence and influence in the household of son, daughters, in-laws and grandchildren were still felt, without her being present.

Mummy loved all her children equally. She kept her family close, always reminding us, Family Is Family. She had saved enough to purchase a piece of rubber estate, somewhere in Segamat, I was not sure where. Mummy explained to us.

* * *

'I have 25 acres of mature rubber trees estate. This is because I have five children and each of you will have a one-fifth share of five acres. There are only five of you. When you look at your hand, there are five fingers, all linked together in one hand. To separate you must cut and that is very painful. Same for this rubber estate, five acres each, all in one property. So everything in fives. All five of you stay together.'

* * *

Mummy was happy with her purchase, her rationale, her life, her family. When my brother and I have families of our own, and looked at our hands, we see Mummy. I have been told the estate has been sold. Period.

Three years passed, and time for me to re-join the harsh reality of leaving home. I left Segamat, with lots of tears, to join my elder brother, two uncles and a cousin in Saint Francis Institution Boarding School, Malacca.

* * *

'Ah Sam, tomorrow your father take you home. Now we eat li.' I felt like it was the Last Supper.

'Ah Por, don't cry. Every holiday I come home to you. My home is here.'

'Ah Kong, why is the holiday so short? I want to stay with you!'

'Ah Sam, you are a young man now. No need to cry. We grow up, we work, we marry, raise a family. This is life.'

* * *

My brother and I had successful careers in Singapore. Then the call came.

* * *

'Ah Sam, you and Pin come, Ah Kong had heart attack.'

* * *

That was uncle, one short sentence.

The news shattered my life. Every Friday, after office, my brother and I drove from Singapore to sit beside him in Segamat hospital, as he had sat beside me when I was a child.

* * *

'Ah Kong, Prof Toh is here to check on you, a second opinion. We take you to Singapore for treatment.' Ah Kong, my Ah Kong, please Jesus please.

'Sam, the damage is severe. I'm sorry,' was Prof's diagnosis.

'Ah Sam, Ah Pin, last night one angel show me five fingers on right hand and two fingers on left hand. I live seven weeks, seven months, seven years I don't know. Ah Sam, Ah Pin, we live we die. Jesus is my friend, I am happy.'

* * *

Those were the last words my Ah Kong said to my brother and me. I was consoled. I had been prepared.

Seven weeks after his heart attack, Uncle called and told me my Ah Kong was with Jesus. My world collapsed – for the first time. I was on auto-mode to return to Segamat with my brother. On arriving, my brother broke into tears and kissed Ah Kong's forehead as he laid on his small bed. I couldn't move or even cry. Though my brother and I were prepared, when it came, it hit us intensely.

I relived the same bad dream when I kissed my brother's forehead one more time. When we buried my brother, I thought I lost my soul mate. I soon had to face another reality, that I lost my soul not my soul mate. Pin Kor, my only brother, the best brother a man could ever have.

I drove on to Uncle's house. After the two demonic floods, Uncle had moved his family further away from the river. No sound was heard. Everyone was asleep, it was still dark. I sat in the car across the road. The house was larger than the shophouse. The kitchen was large. I saw aunties on their stools and me running around.

'Sam don't play with dough! You make it dirty, then you eat!'

Another Hakka staple was *choy-pau-pan,* vegetable dumplings. For Aunties, making *choy-pau-pan* was child's play, but not for Ah Sam to play with. Sum-Ee kneaded rice flour with dribbles of water over a very low charcoal fire. Experience guided her hands on how much water to add. Don't ask her for exact measurements, she had no answer, only, 'Aiyah, just knead and knead, you know ready with your hands.'

I was never allowed to knead the dough over the fire; Ah Por never allowed it. But I helped a lot in making the dumplings. We pinched a ping-pong-ball-sized dough, flattened it in our palms. Why didn't we use the rolling pin? Sum-Ee summed it, 'Aiyah, that way ang moh[24] do, we Hakka do Hakka way.' As the dough was uncooked I could not eat some as I did the peanuts in the *hum-cha* tea.

There were two types of fillings: tiny cubes of *taukwa* or tofu fried with finely chopped leeks and preserved radish, or minced pork fried with leeks and preserved radish. The pieces of *choy-pau-pan* were then steamed for about half an hour and eaten hot with chilli sauce and sweet black sauce. These dumplings were perfect teatime snacks. I could eat twenty of them at one sitting. When I was ready to go home, Aunties would make them and pack them in ice-cream boxes for my brother and me. Again, should they know of anyone going to Singapore, they did the same.

---

24 Literally 'red hair', a local term for Caucasians.

The house was awake. My niece opened the door. Time to move on. I drove on to the small Catholic cemetery. Hearing the haunting horn from that railway track, I paused where my Mummy, Ah Kong, Ah Por, Nee-Ee, Sum-Ee were together in life, together with Jesus. Mummy you left us too soon. We did not know the why, we only knew only the how. The only one who knew would not say. There was no closure for my brother and me. Why did I not bring flowers? Light candles? True love didn't need them.

It was hot and sunny, yet I felt a cold chill. Amidst the tranquillity of the tombstones I cried. I cried for my Mummy, my Ah Kong, my Ah Por, my Nee-Ee, my Sum-Ee, my most beloved brother Pin Kor and perhaps also for myself.

The Men In My Life

Before the days of supermarkets, online shopping, and convenient transport systems of city trains and air-conditioned buses, hawking of foods and goods were the norm. Hawkers travelled on their tricycles, visiting neighbourhoods monthly and calling out their presence. We knew where they stationed themselves and flocked to see what they had to offer. This is the story of the three most looked-forward-to men in my life.

THE MEE TOK TOK MAN

The *Mee*[25] *Tok Tok* man was a showman. The chef enticed us with his *tok tok* invitation. He had a piece of cane bamboo about eight centimetres long split in half. He beat the two pieces against each other to create the *tok tok* melody. It was a musical instrument in itself, depending on the length, thickness, speed and tempo.

We ogled at his offerings. On his pushcart countertop he had a charcoal fire and a small wok, and on the sides plastic double-decker shelves where he displayed his temptations. There were yellow noodles, white flat rice noodles and white rice fine noodles.

---

25 Noodles.

In a plastic container he had his prepared *taugeh*[26], *chai sin*[27] and eggs; in another container he kept the sliced fish cakes and fish balls; in another, ice cubes which itself held a container of cockles; and yet another container of chopped garlic, and of course the must-have pork lard and pork crackers.

The show opened. He tied a Good Morning white towel[28] round his neck to absorb his perspiration. He scooped a tablespoon of the fat, bold and evil, but deliciously guilty, greasy pork lard and loads of cockles into the noodles; the faint yellow flames of the charcoal fire mirrored his equally greasy face and neck. No fried noodles is worth its name without these greasy, tempting lard crackers.

He clanked his metal spatula on his metal wok, belting out in rhythm, 'Come eat, mee soup got, fry also can. Want egg forty cents, no egg thirty cents. Bring own egg also can. *Ta pau*[29] also can. Come!'

At the bottom of his portable kitchen he kept small pieces of charcoal. Beside it he had his cooking oils, several varieties of sauces and chilli paste. His serving plate was the *daun upih*. This is the soft, thin and broad frond sheath of several species of palm tree. The sheath was washed and dried. The durable, pliable, leak-proof reusable sheath was then folded into a boat, the noodles scooped into it and served with a bow. Like a Master Chef, he declared 'I never serve food without tasting it first.' With a nibble of a ribbon of noodle, it passed the 'very good' test. The noodles

---

26 Beansprouts.
27 Mustard leaves.
28 A white face towel with the words Good Morning printed in red on it. It is a favourite towel among vendors.
29 Takeaway.

were best eaten with friends and neighbours around our chef. At times we shared one another's noodles. As a wandering hawker he did not have utensils. Because he was in the premises of his clients, we brought our own utensils and often our own crockery. We were already a 'Reuse, Reduce, Recycle' community back then.

Like all wandering vendors, his charm was his communication and entertaining skills. '*Kuehtau cham-cham mee*, best! You see, mix-mix white and yellow, so nice colour! You want egg, plus 10 cents, all together 40 cents. No egg 30 cents. Bring own egg, free! Also chilli free!' as he clinked-clanked his metal spatula against his wok with a whisk of his wrist. He cleaned his wok with a short broom brush that was all black and greasy and burnt in parts. 'Ah Chek[30], you never wash your wok? Only brush, not clean.'

'Where not clean? Who say! This special secret ingredient, this, the flavour of the noodles. Cannot tell, secret.' I was not quite sure of the secret though. The unmistakable white multi-purpose Good Morning towel round his neck, used to wipe his face, his neck, his hands, and occasionally to cough into, was never removed.

Sometimes he sang his favourite Hokkien[31] songs, complete with gestures, while frying. 'So sad. The Prince is crying because his girlfriend not princess, but poor girl. King and Queen say cannot marry girl, so girl jump into river. Then she become ghost because no one bury her properly. The girl ghost disturb King and Queen, until King say Prince can marry girl. So girl ghost become girl again. Then ghost parents take her away, say ghost girl can

30 Hokkien for 'uncle', and a form of address.
31 A Chinese dialect.

only marry ghost man. So Prince very sad. Ghost girl also very sad. Now I so sad.' He sobbed. His next Hokkien song for us would be six to eight weeks later.

THE MACAM MACAM MAN

The *macam macam*[32] *ah chek* was a travelling hardware-cum-domestic needs salesman who came round every two to three months. He parked himself at a heavy traffic spot, near the little drinks and snacks outlet. He had *macam macam*, all sorts of everything. He rode his bicycle sandwiched between two large carriages, one in the front of the bicycle and another behind the bicycle. Each carriage had four wheels to support the weight of the merchandise. On the outer sides of the carriage he hung his mops, brooms and all other hangables. He honked his little honk, a small, firm rubber like balloon attached to a funnel. Pressing on the balloon created a honk. With a honk and repeated announcements of his new products, he presented himself. He and his carriage were a riot of giddy rainbow colours.

He cycled effortlessly despite the heavy load. The front carriage contained hardware. This included needlework items, lubricating oils, screwdrivers, chair leg caps and tens of other smaller items. He reasoned that sharp or other dangerous items like hammers, knives and scissors were safer to have within sight, lest an unsavoury character spoiling for a fight snatched them. Likewise, small items such as ribbons and raffia rolls could be

---

32 Everything, all sorts (pronounced macham macham).

easily stolen. In the rear carriage he stacked his bigger items: wash basins of all shapes and sizes, buckets, rubber hoses, stools, aluminium utensils – such as plates, bowls, woks, pots, pans and watering cans, all difficult to be stolen unnoticed. He was a sort of today's online retail catalogue. His mission statement, if he had one, would probably read YOU WANT IT – I HAVE IT.

Honk, honk, 'Today got new brooms, just come. Very nice, big, small. Wash floor, sweep floor, garden. See your *longkang* so dirty. Mosquitoes live inside drains, you get malaria, can die. This broom for clean *longkang*. Cheap, cheap only, come see, no buy never mind.'

'Ah Chek, I want zip, long one, you have?'

'Sure got, why don't have? What colour? How long?'

'I want five bamboo poles, to dry clothes.'

'One pole, sixty cents, six, three dollars sixty cents. *Kamsia*, thank you.'

'Blanco, one bottle.'

'Yes, I know. My son school shoes by Friday so dirty. Wash and Blanco clean already.'

'Small plastic chairs, one red and one blue.'

'Skipping rope, and one bag rubber bands, mix colours.' So the purchases went on, bargaining to ridiculous prices, more of a tease, each buyer eyeing what the other bought.

'My friend bought rubber slippers. You got?'

'Ah, Japanese slippers very good to wear. So comfortable. My one good quality, from Japan. Cheap. You very good customer, so I give discount. You tell all your friends come buy. *Kamsia*.

Thank you.'

'Sure or not from Japan. One dollar sixty cents? So expensive!'

Occasionally, there were complaints. A housewife accused him of cheating her into buying a laundry washboard of such cheap quality that it broke when she dropped it. He retorted that she refused to buy the better quality wood board, not his fault, right? He was a walking computer, being able to recall what each customer bought, when and at what price just by deeply eyeing the purchaser. No, you couldn't pull a fast one on him.

Primary school children often sought marbles. He had bags of them, fifty in each bag. 'Ah Chek, fifty too many I want only twenty. Not enough money.'

'You can share with your friend, half-half. Cheaper. You pay fifty cents, your friend pay fifty cents.'

'My friend got already.'

'OK, I teach you business. You buy fifty marbles, one dollar, so one marble only two cents. Then you sell your friend one marble five cents. You sell ten, you get fifty cent, profit already. Good, right?' Small-time schoolkids' businesses sprouted, with rubber bands, sheets of stickers, girly clips.

Another business Ah Chek taught the kids, 'Play *tikam-tikam*[33].'

'How to play?'

The lesson. 'Take twenty pieces of paper this big (showing the palm of his hand). On fifteen paper don't write anything, leave *kosong*, nothing. On one write '1 marble', second write 'ten

---

33 Chance. Here it means a game of chance.

cents', another write 'two rubber bands', another write 'one pencil', and one write 'one more try'. Then fold paper into four, cannot see inside. You sell *tikam-tikam* five cents. Sure make money.'

'What if they complained I cheat them?'

'They cannot complain. *Tikam-tikam* means, play with chance. Sometimes win, sometimes lose.' The first introduction to gambling. Was that entrepreneurial or good business sense, or teaching young children scamming and exploitation of greed?

Nonetheless, he was a welcome ah chek, as we didn't have to go to town for our purchases.

MR POSTMAN

The postman was the only man in my life who wore a uniform. The most anticipated person when you have a penpal. He slotted letters into the red letter box that was nailed in the corner of the front wall of our house. We never knew his arrival as he did not cling-cling or honk his bicycle bell or, in later years, his motorbike horn. He bound his allocation of letters with rubber bands according to the street and in sequence of house numbers.

In the local papers when I was a young teenager, there were two penpal columns –Malaysian penpals and foreign penpals. My first penpal was an Indian girl from Taiping. She was two years my senior. My Sisters-teachers in the convent emphasised a thousand times, *boys do bad things to girls,* so of course penpals had to be girls. It was a four-year penpal relationship. She wrote about the old tin-mining town. She loved the gardens. She studied in the convent like I did. Yes, she had Sisters-teachers. Once I told her that my Sisters-teachers told us that '*boys do bad things to girls*'. She replied, 'I have two brothers and they had never done 'bad things to me'. Sisters have no boyfriends, so they also don't want us to have boyfriends.' Made sense, girlie secret chatter. She, like all convent schoolgirls throughout Malaysia at the time had fifteen minutes of catechism lessons every morning, but her parents did not wish her to attend the Friday twelve o'clock Mass in the convent chapel. She stayed in the library till the end of the school day.

She told me about the tin-mining industry and the rich towkays. 'Our zoo has the endangered Malayan tiger, the only one in Malaysia.' I wanted to be sure, I went to Malacca Zoo. She was right, no Malayan tiger there.

She celebrated the sultan's birthday. She was happy, it was a public holiday. Malacca did not have a sultan, we had a governor. We both celebrated the birthday of the Queen of England, a queen so far away, one whom we would never ever meet in person. But she was so beautiful. I told her I wanted to work in the prime minister's office and get to travel round the world and have tea with the queen in Buckingham Palace. She said she wanted the same too. We described to each other the clothes we would wear, what we would talk about. She would tell the queen about her favourite dosai[34], I would tell her about sambal petai[35]. We were allowed to dream, weren't we?

When she enrolled at Universiti Malaya in Kuala Lumpur,

---

34 An Indian crepe, a favourite breakfast.
35 Particularly smelly local beans cooked in spicy sauce.

she had no time to 'penpal'. We had not met, not even a photo exchanged.

My second penpal was a boy from Kenya. I did not know the gender of people's names as there was no Google search then. I had to buy aerogram air letters. I can't remember how much they cost, probably forty cents. It was a thin lightweight piece of foldable and glued light blue paper for writing a letter to foreign countries. The letter and envelope are one and the same. On one half of the page was a printed stamp in the top right-hand corner. It was the address page. I wrote letters on the other side of the page, folded it into two and continued on the back second half. The small ears along the top and side of the letter were pressed to seal the letter. Mash a little cooked rice with just a touch of water and you get glue.

I told my classmates about my 'Kenyan boyfriend', and we acknowledged he was too far away to do bad things to me. In his first letter he asked whether I was a girl or a boy; he could not tell from my name, so we were on the same page where names were concerned. He lived near a national park and could see Mount Kilimanjaro near the Kenyan side of the border. That rushed us to religiously study the map of Kenya to look for national parks and Mount Kilimanjaro in Philip's World Atlas.[36] But the atlas only displayed a simple map of African political states, natural landscapes and vegetation of mountains and rivers and major

---

36 In secondary school we had Geography lessons. To get out from 'under the coconut shell to learn about the world', our book list included *Philip's World Atlas*. There was no 'Thailand' but 'Siam', no 'Ethiopia' but 'Abyssinia' 'Ceylon' not Sri Lanka, 'Peking' not Beijing, 'Canton' not 'Guangzhou', 'Bombay' not 'Mumbai' and many more.

cities. However, look up Britain, and you got large detailed maps of England, Wales, Scotland and Ireland with their cities and rivers all marked.

My penpal described the animals, and the safaris, his close encounters with elephants. He had bathed in the river with little baby crocs. He told of his rock climbing and hiking adventures, eventually to climb Mount Kilimanjaro. I told him I climbed St Paul's Hill in twenty minutes. He wanted to be a game keeper like his father. 'Save the Elephants'. I wanted to have tea with the queen in Buckingham Palace. He watched a mother giraffe birthing. I collected eggs from chickens in the coop. His favourite food was spiced rice pilaff and goat stew, mine was *nasi lemak*[37] and chicken steamed in Chinese wine. He pounded cassava and corn, I pounded sambal belacan.

His adventures were shared with my classmates; we were envious, we wanted to be Kenyans too. I replied to his letters immediately when I received his. He sent me postcards of Mount Kilimanjaro, rhinos, lions. I sent him postcards of St Paul's Hill, the red Studhuys[38] and satay, meat barbequed over hot embers. As with my Taiping penpal there were no photos sent, only postcards and words to believe in, to savour, to imagine and romanticise and fall in love with.

Many relationships come to a natural end. So did mine with my Kenyan boyfriend. I guess I had nothing of interest to add to his knowledge about my part of my world, so far away. There was nothing he was familiar with: his mother hippos

---

37 Rice cooked with coconut milk.
38 Red building, built by the Dutch when they ruled Malacca, now a heritage landmark.

in the lake, lions hunting for food, the snow-capped Mount Kilimanjaro seen hundreds of miles away. The wait for the postman for his letter was futile after about a year.

The postman was much looked forward to at Christmas and Lunar New Year; how many cards would we receive and from whom? Bills also came in the post, perhaps not so welcome. Unlike all the other men in my life, I still have the postman. I cherish him.

I remember all the men in my life with nostalgia from the days when I was young. Development and progress have and must replace old-school professions. And I accept that.

Teacher, We Ronggeng

I was in the Malaysian education system for 22 years. Newbie teachers were often sent to 'kampong' or village schools. The Chinese schools were mainly in rubber and palm oil plantations, Indian schools in rubber plantations and Malay schools in areas of rice farming. Educational facilities in the 1960s in these schools were few. I was attached to the school in this story for eight weeks for my practicum.

I met the headmaster at the state education office to take me to the school where I was to be attached for eight weeks for my practicum before graduating with a Certificate in Education conferred by the Ministry of Education, Malaysia.

'Follow the road, you see coconut tree trunk painted red, then turn right and the road to school.' What road? There was a *parit* or ditch, and a bridge made of coconut tree trunks spanning the stream. I counted eight trunks tied together with bamboo strips. It was wide and strong enough to take the size and weight of a small car. The bridge was the umbilical cord between the kampong and the nearest town, six to seven kilometres away. We drove between the *batas*[39], through acres and acres of padi fields, left to fallow

---

39 A local Malay term for '*pematang sawah*', the raised ridges between padi fields enabling farmers to walk between fields.

till the clouds decided to shed tears and water the fields, preparing them for rice planting.

Where was the *sekolah*? Finally I found my school. It was an educational shock. Built right in the middle of a cluster of about fifty homes it seemed to me education was the central life of the kampong. A few metres away were two communal wells, one on either side, jealously guarded by all the folks.

The school was an open-plan homemade building – custom-made by the parents. Eight tall coconut-trunk pillars planted deep into the ground and cemented in place supported the roof frame; the roof was made of the large pinnate coconut leaves, woven into a complex and tight-thatched roof. Where were the classrooms? There were four 'rooms', three were classrooms – the first housed Standard[40] 1 (eight pupils) and 2 (nine pupils); the second was for Standard 3 (seven pupils) and 4 (eight pupils); the next was Standard 5 (three pupils) and 6 (eight pupils) – and the fourth room was the staff room. The long desks comprised six coconut trunks sliced lengthwise, cut side up, smoothened and varnished. Coconut stumps supported the desks, and shorter stumps became stools for the children. The staff room was furnished similarly. It was an ingenious way using an abundantly available material: the coconut tree. A mobile chalkboard in each classroom was the only teaching aid. Teachers brought their food and drinks. The fresh breeze cooled us during the hot days; when the rains visited, school was over.

On my arrival I was a curiosity.

The kampong knew I was arriving – the new *cikgu* – to teach

---

40 Primary schools were classified from Standard 1 to 6; secondary schools from Form 1 to 5.

English. There were hushed whispers among pupils and parents who unabashedly stood outside the school to welcome me.

'Good morning, Teacher,' the school chorused. The lesson began, but there were no listening ears, only high-definition surveillance camera eyes scrutinising me inside and outside the school. At the end of the day a parent presented me with two fresh eggs in a woven coconut leaf basket. I was flabbergasted – what did it mean?

The guru besar or headteacher grinned. 'You "pass".' The other teachers nodded. They too had received their two eggs.

'I passed?'

'Yes, you pass, kampong likes you.'

It was a school, a kampong school and a kampong with a difference. Every Friday, the last school day for the week, each teacher received a gift from the kampong: two eggs, a handful of chillies, a cucumber, a young coconut or whatever they had harvested, beautifully presented in coconut leaf baskets. During the fruit season, these wonderful people presented us with a handful of rambutans, a mango, half a comb of bananas, several pieces of jackfruit, guava, a durian and other fruits. They gave from their hearts, not as special requests for favours. I was never to enjoy such hospitality ever again. In return we gifted the children a bar of chocolate, something they could not afford.

One teacher managed two classes in the same room, double tasking, setting a Maths task to Standard 2 while teaching English rubrics to Standard 1. Fifteen minutes later, Standard 1 class practiced the writing, while the teacher checked the Standard 2 Maths. It was the same in the other two classes. The pupils were naturally curious, which was a good thing, and often found the other class's lesson more interesting. They cross-talked and cross-walked. No problem for anyone.

'Ahmad, *mak awak pergi jamban*[41]!' the whole school laughed. The communal village toilets were about twenty metres from the homes, nearer the fruit trees. The call of nature was continuous.

'Rosmah, *mak* dan adik *awak mandi, tak pakai baju!*' a student teased. Rosmah, visibly annoyed and embarrassed, snapped back, 'Your mother and sister also bathe not wear clothes!' Everyone took water from the two communal wells, did their laundry and bathed there, the used water snaking its way to the patch of grass. The women had a sarong tied round their chests, and little ones bathed naked, '*tak pakai baju*'.

'*Mak saya tangkap ayam.*[42]' Mas, pointing to his mum, was happy; there would be chicken for lunch and dinner. Amidst this banter, it was difficult to teach.

At about 11, a student might breathe in deeply, '*Mak saya goreng ikan masin. Sedap*[43].' Somehow the children could identify from whose house the aroma wafted. Everyone breathed in, to savour and indulge in an imaginary lunch of fried salted fish, served with fried onions, fresh red chillies, freshly squeezed limes, and hot rice, and perhaps a fried egg. Perfect silence in that finger-licking meal.

Teaching had its memorable days. The students were easy-going, gregarious and affable, though not so eager to learn.

---

41 Your mum is going to the toilet.
42 My mother caught a chicken.
43 My mother is frying salted fish. Delicious.

Perhaps the syllabus was beyond them or the environment did not motivate them or I was an incompetent newbie or their parents did not see the need for 'very high' education, as they would probably continue to farm the rice fields, cultivate the fruit plantations, tend to a few cows, goats and chickens, and to their vegetable plots; perhaps it was all of the above.

It was a *gotong royong* community. Working together, they had little in terms of urban comforts, but the little was plenty. Water came from the communal wells; light was from kerosene lamps; cooking fuel was dried coconut husks, coconut shell chips and chopped dried tree branches. All fruit trees belonged to the kampong. Vegetables and the animals belonged to individual households. Rice came from their fields. Much of the cooking oil was kampong-produced coconut oil. When the kampong needed other basics like sugar, salt, dried foods, kerosene, additional oil, the village headman took it upon himself to do the shopping in town in his blue Fiat 600. The shopping list was long. All the kids would beg Pak Haji to take them along, *'Pak, saya ikut. Pak, bolehkah saya ikut? Satu kali sahaja.'* They were always unsuccessful; nonetheless there was never a lack of trying. Most of the men had jobs in the towns and proudly rode their Suzuki bikes. They did some shopping for their families. The greatest treat for the kids was a motorbike ride round the kampong. Such simple happiness.

The village headman was addressed Pak Haji, as he had been on the Haj, a pilgrimage to Mecca, one of the tenants of Islam, and on his return he was credited with the title Tuan Haji, and his wife, Puan Hajjah. Tuan Haji was a respected senior but he was addressed affectionately as Pak, father.

Ramadan, the fasting month before Hari Raya Puasa[44] was approaching. The moon was a trace of a sickle. Pak Haji called for a meeting with three strikes on his gong, which was a large frying pan and a wooden spatula. 'The Islamic Council had announced the start of Ramadan. Tomorrow is our first day of fasting.'

The kampong was in festive mood. The first and most important task was preparing coconut oil. I was intrigued, wanting to learn how coconut oil was home-produced.

'How do you make coconut oil, Pak Haji?' I asked.

'*Isi kelapa* plenty protein. You cannot go *jamban*, eat isi, then no problem.' That was a new lesson – the white coconut meat was a remedy for constipation. Pak Haji continued, '*Isi banyak guna – dapat santan*[45], then *rempas* give chicken eat and also use as *baja*, and *sayur* all grow nice. Most valuable is *santan*[46] and oil. Our kampong buys little cooking oil. We make coconut oil, four months, four months we make.'

I was eager to learn. Pak Haji agreed to 'show and tell'. 'I tell you, you still don't know. You must see and help make then you know. But cannot make one day. Must two or three days.'

It was my first stay in a Malay kampong home, and I was honoured to be in the village headman Pak Haji's home.

All houses rested on stilts, either cement or wood. Like all the others, Pak Haji's house had a five-step staircase at the front

---

44 Hari Raya Puasa marks the end of the fasting month of Ramadan. It is a time of forgiveness within the Muslim community and a time for strengthening of bonds among relatives and friends.

45 Lots of uses, especially coconut milk from which you get virgin coconut oil.

46 Coconut milk squeezed from fresh desiccated coconut meat.

of the house from the ground to the living area. There were three bedrooms, a sitting room and a prayer room. On the windows hung pretty lace curtains; the chairs and coffee table had white lace dollies over them. Comfortably seated in a chair, a lazy cat eyed me. 'Comel, sayang,' Mak Hajjah patted her cat. They exchanged love glances. Vases of flowers picked from the garden brightened the rooms. Family pictures reminded them of family togetherness. Her three children worked in Kuala Lumpur, the Malaysian capital. They would be home for Raya. A small Philips portable radio stood proudly on the coffee table.

Another five steps at the back of the rooms led down to the kitchen and dining room. Mak Hajjah's kitchen was immaculate. At one end of the kitchen was the stove and a food cupboard. Beside it was a five-tier wooden rack, each shelf made of strips of wood spaced regularly apart to allow air circulation. The bottom tier kept dried coconut husks, coconut shell chips, dried branches, an iron blowpipe to kindle the fire; the fourth tier was for pots and pans. The third tier supported the rice bin, bottles of cooking oil, dried foods, containers of chillies and all the condiments; the second tier housed the knives, chopping boards, and some kind of pumice stone to sharpen knives. The top tier was covered by a large towel upon which stood a crockery rack and a coconut shell basket for the spoons and spatulas. It had little holes at the bottom to drain the water so the crockery and cutlery were kept dry. Mak Hajjah's kitchen was well stocked with coconut shell utensils, including ladles, spoons, spatulas, soup bowls, moneyboxes and decorative items.

In the middle of the room was the dining table and six chairs;

at the other end, a one-metre-high coconut-thatched enclosure with a waist-high *tempurung*, a clay water container and a wooden lid. Water was brought in from the wells. The enclosure offered privacy if Mak Hajjah chose to bathe at home. Behind the kitchen was a small enclosure where she kept a few chickens.

Beside the bathroom I noticed coconut husks soaked in a large basin of water. '*Mak Hajjah*, why do you soak the husks?'

'*Rendam air*[47] *garam*. Soak in salt water makes fibres loose. Then can make *tali*, ropes, mats and *baju kasar*, rough working clothes when we work in fields.'

The kampong was a picture postcard. All the houses were equally immaculate. The front of every house had flowers of several varieties. Pink, white and red half-metre-tall balsam plants lined the front of the house. At maturity the pregnant pods when gently touched, like a miracle freely gave of their children. By the side of the house were giddily colourful bougainvillea, roses, hibiscus and fauna. Behind the kitchens were the vegetable plots and a good fifty metres away was the large deep compost heap. All the waste, from withered flowers to dead animals, was buried in it with a very slow continuous fire somewhere in its belly, emitting a trail of smoke like Aladdin's magic lamp before the genie made its presence felt. The genie's gift was the rich burnt soil that had produced healthy harvests of long beans, brinjals, gourds, leafy vegetables, chillies and many others, as well as for the flowering plants. There was enough good soil for everyone. When the sweet potato or tapioca tubers were harvested, the kids shafted some into the compost in the evenings. The next morning

---

47 Pronounced 'eye-eh'; water.

my pupils took me by the hand to the compost heap for breakfast. 'Teacher, *ubi*, sweet potato. Very good to eat. Sweet.' As they dug in, I could have sworn it was on top of the charred remains of an animal, probably a cat! The tubers were not wrapped in foil or in banana leaves – nothing. The kids delightfully *'hooo-hoooed'* the ash off and bit into them. I did the same. Everyone had their fill.

'What are the things we get from the coconut tree, Mak Hajjah?'

The kids intercepted me, 'Cikgu, we *boleh* get toddy from *bunga kelapa*[48]. But Muslims, toddy *haram*[49]. Pak Haji *tahu siapa* making or drinking toddy, he report police.' The sap of the flower can be boiled to make syrup. The syrup is processed and fermented to produce alcohol or vinegar, but here alcohol was out of the equation. The water of the young fruit is the purest and most health benefitting water. It provides hydration for the body and natural cleansing of the kidney. The tender white meat melted in your mouth. Adding ice cubes and a slice of lemon would be nice, I thought to myself.

It was coconut harvesting and coconut oil making weekend. After breakfast of *kopi* and *nasi goreng*, rice fried to perfection with eggs, *sambal*[50], and freshly harvested cucumbers, the kampong was ready to work. All the basins, pails and pots were brought out. Like a colony of ants, everyone knew their role in the scheme of kampong life. With the agility of monkeys, young men climbed the coconut trees to harvest the nuts. They had coconut fibre ropes loosely tied round their legs to sort of hop up. They

---

48 Flowering fronds of the coconut.
49 Forbidden to Muslims.
50 A spicy condiment.

wore the coconut husk fibre work clothes, a small machete slipped into their pants. The matured nuts rained down like wartime parachutists into enemy land.

It was conveyor belt activity. The older children delivered the nuts to a group of men who deftly husked them with an upright iron spike; a group of women cracked the shell with a small machete and drained the water into large basins, then another group grated the meat from the shells with a simple foot-pedal grater. They did this in turns, as there were about five hundred coconuts. Another group of women squeezed the milk out using a *sarong* – a woman at each end twisted the sarong in opposite directions, then added a little water for the second squeeze. They were happy, singing and telling stories, some of which I suspected were raunchy, as the kids were shooed off to some task, after which there were peals of naughty laughter and singing and slapping and pinching of one another's body parts. Seeing me guessing their laughter, one explained, 'This hard work, *mesti nyanyi* songs, *cerita* stories. *Kalau tidak*, how to work?' The others nodded. '*Cikgu, cuba lah*, come help.' I did not realise the strength needed to twirl the sarong to squeeze the milk out. The *santan* was strained through another sarong. Each family took several basins of the precious milk home and left them aside overnight.

The next morning, together with the call of the roosters, Pak Haji hit the *gerengseng*, the large bronze cauldron with his paddle sticks and his voice boomed, '*Bawah santan!*' The women brought their basins. Overnight the *santan* had split into cream floating on the water. We gently scooped the cream into the three *gerengseng*, each supported on three large rocks. The water was kept aside to water the vegetables, 'Banyak vitamins for *tamanan*,' Pak Haji explained. Pak Haji had prepared the slow coconut-husk fire that had to be constantly fed by the children. Adults with paddles took turns to gently stir the cream, till it turned into oil. It was extremely exhausting. After four to five hours, the cream had transformed into beautiful clear aromatic oil. The bits of brown residue were gently scooped out and later used as garnishes.

Now it was time for sharing the oil. Each family brought bottles of various shapes and sizes. Pak Haji scooped a cup and with a funnel poured it into each bottle – one for you, one for you, one for you until all families had one cup. Then the second cup, the third, fourth until ninth, until there was not enough to share. It was poured into several small bottles and kept aside to prepare *nasi kunyit*, *rendang*, *sayur lemak* and other delicacies for Hari Raya celebrations. Everyone was happy.

The next day the women invited me to learn everything that could be made from coconuts. '*Cikgu tak tahu apa apa, jadi pastikan sahaja, kemudian belajar.*' Yes I admitted I didn't know anything, and learning began with watching then doing.

A few young men had climbed the trees and tapped the nectar from the flowering frond. Two grandmothers were lighting a dried coconut-husk fire under a large pot supported on three large rocks, to make *gula kelapa merah*, coconut brown sugar favoured in *kueh*, our variety of local cakes. I watched the process. It was not easy. The women continuously stirred the nectar over a very low fire until it turned shiny golden and viscous. They whipped it quickly to cool it then poured it into bamboo moulds. The *acuan* or moulds were cut so the bamboo nodes formed the base. There were long thin moulds, short stumpy ones, tiny ones. When the *gula* hardened the women gave the mould a sound beating on all sides and, plop, out dropped the *gula*. Again there was much regaled laughter. A woman cheekily teased, '*Ini dia*!' referring to appendages I guessed. Others joined in, '*Manis kah? Sedap ya? Bagus ya? Cukup kah? Besar sekali!*' Sweet? Nice? Good? Enough? Large? The banter was all in good fun.

'Our *gula* very good, best in Malaysia. Money good. Pak Haji sell and buy soy sauce, salt, pepper, kerosene for us,' the women boasted. 'You make *kueh-kueh*, best, *tentu sedap sekali*. All people like. Best!'

I was curious why the children were collecting the exposed roots of the coconut tree. Pak Haji explained, '*Kita keringkan*. When very dry we keep. If your skin itchy, you got fever, go *jamban* many many times, or stomach not good, then boil *akar*, then not so hot, drink. You become good already. If mouth also got *sakit*, very pain, boil and wash mouth, become good.' The kampong cherished their coconut trees. It is the only tree I know of where every part has value. Pak Hajji promised he would showcase all the things that could be made from every part of the tree.

After the afternoon siesta the village was alive again. I sat with the women, busy weaving handicrafts all made from some part of the coconut. '*Cikgu*, want learn? I show make *sarong ketupat*[51],' the women volunteered. First came the leaves. As a beginner, I split the large pinnate into individual leaves, then split the leaves from the spine. It was more difficult than when I observed the children doing it.

---

51 Woven palm leaf pouch. Ketupat is boiled rice in the sarong.

'Cikgu, *tarik* slow, *tak putuskan.*' I had to ensure the little knife was along the spine and drag it down slowly. Finally I got it, a one to eight yield compared to my pupils. The children collected the spines to dry, then bundled them together into brooms.

Without eyeing but with slithering fingers the women deftly wrapped two pieces of leaves round their palms, weaved here and there and *wahlah*: a *ketupat* pocket was born, ready to receive the rice grains within its belly and be boiled into ketupat, rice cakes eaten with satay, *sayur lodeh* and other traditional celebratory dishes. The little children sat at their parents' feet and learnt the art. There were tons of leaves, so trial and error was encouraged.

I repeated slowly, 'Two leaves, wrap them onto your palm. Place the left side leaf on top of the right one. Then from the right side, insert the leaf from beneath the first checked line. Repeat until I use all 4 wraps.' Work stopped as the audience watched me struggle – top right, crossed, checked, insert, now insert where again? I was frustrated, but it was good entertainment for all. Jeynab, my Primary 3 pupil, offered: '*Cikgu* I *ajar* you. Now I teacher, you *murid.*' Yes, a teacher does not know everything, there were many things my pupils could teach me. Well, I did eventually manage to weave a few square ketupat, while the experts did rectangular, triangular, diamond-shaped and even bird-shaped ones!

Another group of children and women weaved the leaves into table baskets for fruit, eggs, spools of thread and needles and other knick-knacks; they folded pretty art pieces like chickens, flowers and insects, and strung them together into mobiles which were hung on the verandas; women weaved them into fans, hats, lamp shades, bracelets, headbands, rings and necklaces and little anklets for the babies. These Pak Haji sold in town before Hari Raya.

We had a feast that evening – a breaking of fast. The school desks became the grand dinning tables. The women brought out their beautiful sarong batik as tablecloths, each section with different designs and colours. In the *gerengseng* we fried *ikan bilis*, and sambal belacan fried rice, the anchovies added crunch; *sayur lemak* enriched with freshly squeezed *santan* and beef *rendang*. It was the largest communal campfire meal I had attended. With a little prodding, the coconut husks, dried twigs and leaves generously gave of their popping laughter and light to illuminate the cool evening. The children ran around and played. After dinner, folks brought out their *jembe* drums, gongs, aluminium basins, pots with lids and sticks and together they made music. What madness I thought, making music with a potpourri of kitchen utensils, but there was method in their madness. It was the original full orchestra, each 'instrument' knew its part.

Later, Pak Haji fetched his Philips radio and inserted his cassette tape of popular songs. He held up a packet of twelve new batteries, enough battery power for the evening. The spontaneous request, '*Burung Kakak Tua*' by Anneka Gronloh, was played repeatedly. Grandmothers smiled toothless smiles and sang along, it was their song, '*Nenek sudah tua, giginya tinggal dua*'[52]. Anita Sarawak, Sharifah Aini, P Ramlee crooned the evening away. The beat enticed the folks, young and old to *ronggeng* and *joget*, popular Malay dances.

---

52 'Grandmother is old, only two teeth left'; lyrics from 'Burung kakak tua'.

My pupils egged me, 'Cikgu, teacher, we *ronggeng lah, sama sama.*'

'Cikgu, I you *ronggeng* ok?' and Mazlan cheekily took my hand and gyrated to P Ramlee's *'Bujang Lapok'* and *'Do Ray Me'* – both award-winning hit songs.

I was fooled by the slow-paced beat and rhythm of the *ronggeng* and happily joined the women. The music was catchy, and as hands and legs swayed, so did the hips with turns and twirls. The younger folk unabashedly strutted their stuff, not unnoticed by Pak Haji and his wife. When Pak Haji thought the gyrates were several too many, and hips were touching hips, he beat the gong, announcing, 'We work very hard make coconut oil, cook *makanan*, dancing, time to go home and sleep, we work some more tomorrow.'

They begged, but Pak Haji was adamant. Only with the grandmothers' appeal – *'Satu lagi,* "Burung Kakak Tua", *kita pun tua, ta' ada gigi'* – did he relent. *'Satu kali sahaja.'* Everyone sang the last song of the evening with such gusto I wondered whether the next village would be awakened.

The weekend was over. It was time to go to bed and be ready for school the next day. I had a room in the front veranda on Pak Haji's home. In the freshness of the night air, the crickets chirped, the leaves rustled their lullabies and I fell into peaceful slumber.

'Cikgu, *ronggeng bagus ya? Mahu ronggeng lagi?* I want some more,' Mona asked me the next morning.

'Can you speak in English, please?'

The class roared, actually the whole school roared. Silly request, why ask a question when I already knew the answer?

'Teacher *ronggeng* dance very good. You want *ronggeng* I more?'

'Yes, I do. I enjoyed it very much, thank you. Now we do spelling.'

'Cikgu, you *ronggeng* me, *boleh*? Can? I very good.' Sirul jumped up on the desk to *ronggeng* and soon the whole school was ronggeng-*ing*. Pak Haji appeared. Without a word, discipline was restored, lessons continued. I was sure I was teaching, not sure though there was learning, amidst the *ronggeng* and Anneka Gronloh and P Ramlee belting their songs in the silence that followed. Nonetheless the eyes, the smiles, the body movements spoke volumes and loudly too, in perhaps not so childish innocence.

That Friday, Mak Hajjah gave the guru besar and teachers a small bottle of coconut oil. She explained the beauty secrets of coconut oil. 'As hair oil hair very shiny. *Kalau* put on face every day, no wrinkles. See I sixty-two years skin so *cantik*, Pak Haji say my face so beautiful.' She sensuously stroked her face and neck, cackled with laughter, a wink in her eyes. 'I drink one spoon morning, so my body clean, toilet no problem.'

'Mak Hajjah, how do you know this?'

'My mother teach me. Her mother teach her. Her mother mother teach her. Now I teach you, and all the people in kampong.'

That weekend I viewed kampong life with new eyes. I had wondered how they managed without showers in the privacy of bathrooms, ice-cream on hot afternoons, and electricity. Then again how would they yearn for something they never had? They had their natural air-conditioned homes. The cool breeze sailed effortlessly through the open doors and windows; fellowship versus privacy; ice-cream stored perhaps for months in some dark, dank warehouse cold room versus freshly made *kueh-kueh* to be shared. There was never a need for padlocks, only a latch and that too, to secure the doors and windows from the wind. They had survival skills, living skills, social skills, community living skills, loving skills, happiness skills. Theirs was the good life, in the kampong without the interference of modern concepts of a good life.

Decades later, many tycoons, popularly celebrated as 'captains of industry', would seek refuge in the very same environment they had destroyed, now a back-to-nature retreat, available at a premium. 'Progress' had stolen the ways of the kampong, and the 'progress-*ers*' in their later years would seek the serenity of kampong life. There might no longer be any kampong life as it once was. The present shamelessly advertised 'Relax, Enjoy the Simple Ways of Kampong Living' getaways are artificially created by other 'captains of industry' – the kampong life with modern amenities. I was fortunate to have lived the genuine kampong life, if only for eight weeks in 1966.

You Might Want
To Marry My Husband

The premise of this story is based on true events, but the
narrator is a man whose wife is sick. My husband passed
away at 54, of cancer. He was concerned about my well-
being. He said that I should not wallow in widowhood.
I am a widow, twenty-three years on. How does one un-
love a much-loved spouse?

That's what my wife said. Verbatim. You might want to marry my
husband. Not you as one particular woman, but her single and
available women friends. Trusted girlfriends she grew up with,
played with, went to school with, who have remained BFF – Best
Friends Forever.

I am lost for words when I first heard her say it to her
widowed elder sister. Her sister and I are aghast; the cancer has
created hallucinations that we are having an affair. She justifies
her appeal. We know she's dying, lying in the hospice from Easter
and now it's Christmas. She reprimands us, let's not play word
games, all those clichés, '*You'll soon be on your feet, believe me.*'
No, she doesn't believe us or anyone else. We don't believe it

either. She claims doctors are pathological liars with C patients. I would not go that far. Doctors give hope, I believe.

It happens when her BFF visit, the single ones. They are confused, uncomfortable, eyeing me suspiciously. I suspect she widens her net in case her sister and I have no fondness for each other, are too familiar with each other, think the relationship is somewhat weird.

'My love, please, you are going to get well. Your friends are uncomfortable when you say that. I feel embarrassed, it might appear I will forget you and find comfort in another woman's embrace. I love you. Forever.'

'Darling, I don't want you or anyone to mourn my passing. We have had twenty-five happy years, just you and me. And sister.'

'My love, please, Dr Raj is the top oncologist. We have him.'

She smiled. Was it a smile? Or a snigger, an acceptance of her disease? I do not know.

Where are we now? We are in the prime of our lives, she is fifty-one, a successful interior decorator, and I, at fifty-two, run a successful travel agency. Her sister lost her husband in an accident just three years into their happy married life. She now works in my agency. We are a threesome. So, to my wife it's perfectly natural that her sister and I marry, after her passing, of course.

I need an explanation for this strange behaviour. I need an explanation for her sister and her BFF to whom she has made such a proposition.

In her hospice bed, she explains, 'Things happen, people change, but life goes on. A death of a spouse is a loss, sure, it is a loss. But grieving doesn't help one to live. Life is meant to be lived, to be happy, to enjoy companionship. We've had a good twenty-five years, a quarter of a century together. I've always been happy with you. Are you hap ...?' She dozes off, too tired to continue. The big C makes its presence felt as it had for over twenty years.

She asks me my purpose in life.

'To love you and be with you.'

'Wrong answer,' and laughs like a child whose trick question baffles her friends. 'Try again.'

'To love you and care for you and be with you always.'

She laughs. 'Almost correct answer.'

'Be with you always.'

'As till ... when? Say it, my darling,' she pleads. 'Say it, as in our marriage vows.'

'Till death do us part.' She clasps my hand, smiles and is happy I get the answer 'right' – 'Till death do us part.'

She cringes in silent pain. I feel helpless, nothing I can do to ease her pain. I feel abandoned, how could she leave me in the prime of our lives? I study her, to internalise what she says. Can one love a DECEASED? Does one cease loving a DECEASED? Can one *un*-love a much-loved spouse? Can one love another all over again, after an intense love affair with a spouse? Can one, can I love another woman with the same intensity and passion as I love my wife? I do not know, and not until my wife is a 'DECEASED', maybe.

How do I love my wife? By her bed, monitoring the machines recording her heartbeat, her blood pressure, the silent drips of the liquid antibiotic and painkillers slowly easing their way into her system, the urinal bag hanging on the inner side of the bed, a receptacle for pale orange fluid with blots of blood. Every now and then she opens her eyes. I hold her hand. She smiles. She does not laugh much now. She smiles. She nudges me, 'My love, go home, sleep. You are tired. I am fine.' No, she is not fine. Her lips do not say the pain she is suffering. Her face does, despite her smiles. I remember a poem I learnt in school, about loving – how many ways can one love. Can we count the ways we love? The different kinds of love? Can't remember it.

She whispers a request, 'Tell our love story.'

She loves our love story. With every retelling it becomes more magical, the 'I love you' more intense. Our love story ... where do I begin? She whispers again, 'I want to die in a love story'.

My wife is a happy woman, never saying a harsh word to anyone. We meet at our university freshmen dance. She catches my eye, standing alone in her red dress, a purple sash, a green scarf with orange polka dots, and yellow shoes.

'Hi, I'm Jason.' She laughs, I think, for no apparent reason. It is contagious, I laugh, too. I mutter, 'Interesting dress sense.'

She laughs again. 'I'm planning a career in interior design, so I'm playing with colours, designs, to gauge responses. Do you like it?'

'Yes, I do.'

She laughs, 'You are lying. I read minds.'

'What am I thinking now?'

Unabashedly, she holds my hand, and giggles, 'You are attracted to me, and I like you. What do you do?'

'I am into the travel industry.'

'Great! We will make a perfect match. I will offer my interior design skills to hotels, motels, restaurants, pubs and cafés; you will bring in tourists to these establishments. Our company will be J and J, Jason and Juliet. Wonderful!'

We plan our dreams. She does part-time work at cafés, pubs, restaurants, hotels, motels. She talks to patrons about what attracts them to food and beverage outlets. Is it the décor, the food, the beverages, the hospitality of service staff? She writes the responses in her notebook. I do part-time work in travel agencies, to learn advertising, securing hotel rooms, budgeting, and organising inbound and outbound tours. When we graduate we have a good idea of what makes good business plans. We marry right after graduation; pursue our dreams. Within six years we set up J and J Travel Agency for mid-budget travellers. We are happy.

We want a family. Not successful. Medical tests confirmed the big C of the womb. The operations save her; they also confirm we are not to be parents. That has not stopped her loving and enjoying our nieces and nephews, growing with them into adults.

'We have the best of parenthood. No diapers to change, no sleepless nights, no worries about allergies, schoolwork, friends, teenage angst, boyfriends, girlfriends. As aunt and uncle we have the privilege to spoil them, just a little.' A tinge of sadness in her gentle voice.

Not true. We change diapers, talk to their friends, worry as parents of teenagers. We spoil them in grand ways.

My wife and I spend weekends with her sister and her husband. The sisters are soulmates, chattering and whispering and giggling and casting side glances at us two husbands.

'You are bitching about us. We are bitching about you too,' I tease. We laugh and go out for pizza and beer.

My wife quivers. Her sleep is restless, her breathing heavy, at times she grasps for breath. 'Water please,' she murmurs. 'More water, please.' The water spills over her lips, she doesn't drink. Or she can't drink. I don't know.

Water. I remember our first cruise, compliments of the cruise operator, Star of the Sea. My tour groups are regular clienteles. We have a private suite, a room with a view of the rolling waters and the sky from here to eternity.

Some kids at the next table at breakfast are sharing what they see from their porthole rooms right in the belly of the ship. 'We see fishes, octopus, sharks, whales, and Ariel. She's so beautiful, so graceful, long brown hair and a gorgeous blue tail. Wish I could swim with her.'

'I want to see mermaids, too, and mermen as well.' We request for a porthole room in the belly of the ship.

The captain finally gives in; he, too, wants to see mermaids and mermen. One of the galley staff has to give up his room for the night. No mermaids, no mermen, no whales, no octopus, no sharks, no fishes, no nothing. She laughs, then, feels sad for taking over the cramped room for staff. She leaves a comfortable tip under the pillow.

Her sister and I sit by the hospital bed watching her, loving her, dying with her. Am I, 'I', without her? She, our lifeline of happiness, and I and her sister, being, doing, living, together.

It startles me that she reads my thoughts, 'Are you happy my love?' she asks, what she has never asked. 'Be happy. We have done lots of fun things, the travels, the friends, and all that. But happiness is not just doing fun things, it is doing meaningful things as well.' The big C is raising its frightening, ever-growing tentacles to devour the colon, stomach, liver, slowly sucking its way, one sucker after another.

I feel guilt. Is it me that had created the stress that resulted in the C? That one time I had insisted she accompany the outbound group to Korea, as she speaks enough Korean. It was 'A Korean Winter' package. She was recovering from flu. She returned home coughing and feverish. It was a severe case of flu leading to pneumonia. I feel directly to blame for her sickness, that I didn't do enough to help her when she became ill.

'What do you like to do, something meaningful, my love?'

'I can't do it, you have to do it for me. Stamps, the stamps.' I receive hundreds of mail from all over the world. She carefully cuts out the corner of the envelopes with the stamps, soaks them in water, and dries them. They are neatly enveloped in the pages of the stamp albums, a cupboard full in our home office. The stamps are her children, she says, and they are great investments. I love her too much to argue the futility of keeping such common stamps. What am I to do with them?

Then she asks her sister, 'Are you happy?' Her sister's deep river of tears flows in silence, in love and in pain. She touches her heart. 'My heart is a pocket where I keep all my loved ones.'

My wife smiles, 'I have a large pocket too, to keep all my loved ones. I've sealed my pocket.'

What now my love? How does one live on without a soulmate?

'Darling, you are the sole decision maker of what to do with my ashes. I love you and trust you will know what to do with me as a "DECEASED".'

I wish she would tell me what she would like. I feel burdened, guilty I may be doing the 'that's not what I wish'. Does she know my thoughts and feelings when I am 'single and available' as she puts it, when proposing 'You may want to marry my husband' to her BFF, and in particular to her sister? Does she think I will get over her after it's all over, and cast my desires elsewhere? I am angry imagining she thinks that of me. Is that her intent? Or that she thinks I am not able to be alone.

Her sister and I talk. 'What is it like to live alone, to sleep alone, be alone, eat alone, feel alone?' I ask.

'I'm never alone, lonely sometimes when I lost my soulmate,' she replies, looking me straight in the eyes. 'We're born alone, we live alone, we die alone. But I am never alone. I had my husband and her and you. Are you alone?' Gently she touches my hand.

'I don't know.'

'It's good for a person to spend time alone now and then. It is an opportunity to discover who you are without her. Maybe someday you will meet someone who actually complements your life and makes it enriching again.'

'And you, what about you? Have you someone?'

'Have you decided what to do with her ashes?' She avoids the question.

'We'll scatter her ashes in the sea.'

'She would like that, set her free to roam the seven seas, the free spirit she always is.'

'The stamps. She has each country stamp in plastic bags to be given to the Philatelic Society. To be auctioned or sold and proceeds to Cancer Research.'

My wife smiles. She is happy the stamps issue is settled.

I watch my wife smile in her sleep. Is it sleep, as the sleep people do at night in bed? Or is she passing in and out between living and dying? I study her face, pale; her eyelids fluttering as in disturbed slumber; her mouth cringes: her breathing laboured.

She whispers, 'At my funeral I want everyone to wear white please. White, pure like a cloud, floating high in the sky. I want everyone to let go of me like a cloud, transient.' It takes me a long time to grasp what she says. It is hard to believe that she who is so important to me is not coming back.

What she says next makes me cringe. 'Darling, OK if I have a small church service?' I am numbed, shocked. Religion has not been a part of my life, and I never thought she is religious either. I do not know her as well as I thought.

'Do you know?' I demanded of her sister. 'Why didn't you tell me? Secret visits to church? A conspiracy against me?'

'The spouse is the soul of the other. Look into her personal drawer.'

There is a handheld, worn-out bible, many passages highlighted. Psalm 23 and Psalm 91 completely highlighted in yellow. What else do I not know? I feel pain and distress. How do I not know? Why did she not tell me? I hear her whisper, 'I love you my darling.' Does loving mean denying one's needs? It is a frightening thought I might have been selfish, or blind, living in a different world.

I feel anger. I feel angry towards her, dying before her time. I feel angry for things we did or didn't do. I feel angry she might not have told me all of her needs. What do I want, need, to say to her, in the middle of the night? As if she reads my thoughts, she whispers, 'My darling, I love you till death do us part. Please my darling, be happy no more pain for me. We have been happy. Live for me.'

I remember the kind of life she wanted for me, a happy life. What kind of life does she want? Have I ever asked her? There is much longing to tell her how sorry I am, not understanding her needs. I wanted to cry, but the tears refuse to flow. Why am I speechless?

She holds my hand tight, 'Hug me.' I call her sister, she wants her sister here. Her sister wants to be here. We sit on either side of the bed. We hold hands, as in a triangle, a sort of Holy Trinity.

I fall asleep. Her sister shakes me awake. My wife is smiling, her eyes bright, open. She asks for apple juice. She turns to me, 'Kiss me my darling. I love you.' She turns to her sister, 'Kiss me my darling, I love you.' She clasps my hands to those of her sister, tells us to be happy, and bids us goodbye.

Kamani

Kamani was my Sri Lankan live-in domestic help (DH) in Singapore for 14 years. DHs were mainly Sri Lankans, Filipinas and Indonesians. They were poor and had little education. All came to Singapore to work as DHs to support their families at home.

Yes, madam. No, madam. Thank you, madam.

That was twenty-year-old Kamani when she first stepped into my house in 1984. The first time out of her comfort zone, a small village somewhere in the middle of Sri Lanka, not even noted in *Philip's Atlas of the World*, an eleven-hour bus ride to Colombo to board a plane to a strange new place called Singapore. She was neatly dressed in a billowing ankle-length green skirt, a matching loose long-sleeve blouse that reached to her calf and a scarf thrown over her shoulders, and sandals.

Fourteen years later: 'Madam, when I reach Cyprus I telephone you. And madam, I very happy to work in your house. Thanks for presents and everything.' She returned the piece of jade pendant; her mother would see it as some valueless green stone and might throw it out. She hugged me, both of us fighting tears and then she was gone, gone from my household, my life.

What was it like to work in an unknown country, for an unknown employer, in an unknown culture and environment, with unknown work specifics? Her home agent had given her two postcards, one of the Singapore Botanic Gardens and the other of Orchard Road.

At my first meeting with Kamani, she courted me with her unblinking, huge, wide eyes, which revealed her fears and sudden loneliness in her strange new home, yet they seemed to challenge me. They seemed to say in a defiant way, probably to herself, 'Well, this is the path I have chosen, and it *is* the right path.' She held tightly on to her small well-worn brown tote bag, containing all her worldly possessions: four changes of clothes, some personal toiletries, a prayer book and a small statue of Lord Buddha. In sign language she told us Lord Buddha would take care of her, and nothing bad would happen.

Kamani was a petite girl, and her glossy black hair streamed down to her waist. No, her hair was never to be cut, only trimmed, her mother and grandmother had made her promise. It was neatly braided, into one long plait and twirled round into a neat bun with a blue ribbon interwoven into it, just above the nape. Within a week, she asked in sign language if she could pick a flower from one of my plants and decorate her hair with it. Her love for flowers, plants and gardening soon manifested itself when she took it upon herself to do the gardening, in the little garden that I had. Her high cheekbones perfectly matched her oval-shaped face. When she smiled, which she seldom did for the first six months, her beautiful white teeth glowed against her dark skin.

The first few months were difficult. She had never ever slept alone in a room, and for a while she slept with granny. We had communication problems, food problems, hygiene problems, and lots more problems. She had wanted to go home, but she had debts, and her family had strongly objected to her working abroad. She would face the wrath of her parents and be scorned by neighbours. No one in her village had been tempted by the recruiting agents' promises of earning 'good money' in Singapore, leading to a luxurious life for the family, and an opportunity to 'see the world'. The closest to seeing the world among her village community was the headman, when he went to Colombo for a meeting. He had captivating stories to tell, of moving staircases, where one had to only stand on a step and be moved up or down; of drinks in cans coming out of a huge box by the wall when a coin was put in; of the little box-like handheld 'thing' which switched the television on and off as well as to change channels, and many more. Kamani was mesmerized, wanting to see the world. She had insisted on going with the agent, and in return for her parents' blessing, had promised them money to cement the mud floor of their house; to 'bring electric inside house'; to buy cows; a motorbike for father to sell the milk from the cows; for mother the gold chain she had yearned for, and many other promises. The fear of shame should she go home so soon was so devastating she decided to stay on. We had a translator, an Indian woman who worked in the agency that recruited Kamani, so we did 'talk'.

She questioned, 'Wash rice so many times? Wash one time can already.' 'Where got so many water? Why must pay water? We take well, no pay money.' 'Machine wash clothes? How machine know wash?' 'Flush toilet, waste water only. Dig hole and bury. Then vegetables all grow so nice.' 'How can body wash make body clean? Only soap make floor, plates, body, hair, window, dogs all clean.' Then one day she said, 'So hard!' Two years later she reminded me that even though she had said 'So hard!' back then, it was no longer so. She enjoyed the hot shower, the convenience of the gas stove, the ice cubes in her ginger tea on hot afternoons. She experienced riding the escalator, the remote control of the television set, the drinks vending machine and marvelled at the ATM, 'How money come out machine, who put money inside?'

The Singapore agent spoke to her three times a week in the first two months to ensure she had settled in. In her first month I asked her, in sign language and with materials, 'Kamani, do you want to write a letter to your parents?'

'No, madam. Thank you, madam. I tell agent, agent tell Sri Lanka agent, he tell my father. Everything good. Father got madam house number, telephone number. There, no post office. One man come to shop when got many letters for people. Father said no write. Lord Buddha take care of everything.'

Her first meal with me was chicken *briyani*[53], as I thought she would be familiar with the dish. She couldn't eat it, never saw it before. Butter? Kaya[54]? 'No, madam.' Most foods served were returned with, 'No, madam. Thank you, madam.' She relished her dhal, tomatoes, and bean curry and so we ate Sri Lankan

---

53 Biryani is popular throughout the Indian subcontinent, as well as among its diaspora. It is a mixed rice dish made with Indian spices, rice, and meat and vegetables.
54 Local coconut jam.

food, very simple but very good and very healthy. I watched her preparing her favourite chickpea curry.

Her deft fingers sliced a small onion, a green chilli, tore two sprigs of curry laves, broke four dried chillies into pieces, measured a teaspoon of mustard seeds, cumin seeds. It was difficult to make her understand that the onion, chillies, and curry leaves had to be washed. In sign language she said, 'No wash madam. No wash.' I did not cherish Serangoon Road dust and creepy crawlies in my food. She had boiled the chickpeas the night before and they were soft and ready to cook. She heated the oil and fried the curry leaves.

I surprised myself how we could communicate and understand each other with a smattering of English and Sinhalese and finger work. Into hot oil toss the curry leaves. She smiled, thumbs up. It was so aromatic. In went the onion and salt. 'Onion soft, madam.' She added the chillies, cumin, mustard seeds. Her fingers jumped and her voice went pop-pop, pointing to the seeds. 'Now chickpeas go inside, some grated coconut go in. Cook not so long. All cook already.' Pointing to her mouth, '*puri*[55].' In my home we ate rice.

We learnt from each other. We also needed the translator fewer times.

'Kamani, this letter is for you.' With excitement she read it. 'Madam, everyone good. Father ask money some more. The money agent give all finish already, agent take some money. Father said send post office money. Post office keep money. Not money,

---

[55] Puri is a deep-fat fried bread made from unleavened wholewheat flour.

money, madam. Money money never get.' And so the bimonthly Post Office order was religiously observed.

'Madam, contract near finish. Madam still want Kamani? But I go home first.' That was Kamani's first trip home, for three weeks, after two years.

'Did you have a good time with your family Kamani?'

'No, madam. At airport my family wait me. I so happy. There also one man I don know. My mother very angry I wear jeans. When reach home, she beat me. She take jeans and cut and cut and cut. Sisters and brothers all cry. The man just sit there. Then he go home. Morning come my mother say I no work in Singapore. I marry that man. But I don want. I keep passport in body. Nobody can get. Mother everyday scold. I tell madam keep money. I no go back, madam take money.' So she continued her stay with me. We were comfortable with each other. She was eager to learn my cuisine.

'Madam, my father put floor in house. Red cement, very nice.' 'Madam, my house now got electric lights. Mother very, very happy.' 'Madam, my father buy TV. Now no go shop. Other people come watch TV, give father some money, like shop, but less little bit. Father said some people no pay, stand outside window watch. Cannot close window, very hot.' 'Madam, my father buy two cows. Cows very good. Milk sell get money. Cows marry got baby, some more cows.'

'Madam, shop near my house got telephone. I tell shop man what time I telephone, my family wait talk to me. Madam, I use your telephone can?

'Madam, sister marry that man. Mother say I don want marry

him, marry sister. I happy my sister marry. Mother ask buy so many things, sister marry must give many, many things. Buy gold chain, thick one, one hand long. Also must buy for mother-in-law, mother, grandmother. Sari, three sari sister wear marry, two give mother, two give mother-in-law, two give grandmother, one sister one and sister-in-law one. No need give presents. Mother say this give enough.'

'That's a lot of money, Kamani.'

'Yes, Madam, I know. No buy everybody angry.'

We went to Serangoon Road[56] shops and noted the prices of saris and gold. 'Madam, mother ask why money so many. Only buy give sister gold, two sari, mother one, mother-in-law one and grandmother one. Other people no need.'

'Madam. I no go home after contract, can?'

The standard guidelines was to give her the price of the airfare and three weeks salary.

'Brother want buy motor. Now got four cows got plenty of milk, got motor, brother sell more easy. I want buy gold chain, one bangle and one ring. I don have gold. Only buy for sister marry. Madam, family always ask for money. Now sister go hospital got baby, husband no money pay hospital.'

She decided that she would save more for herself, and send one month's salary quarterly, to her parents. The milk was bringing in a good income.

Eight years later, she decided to take her second trip home. 'Madam, mother so happy I going home. I go Deepavali. Five days enough madam. Mother find man tell me marry. I don want.

---

56 An Indian enclave with Indian restaurants, clothes shops and
   jewellery shops.

Madam, you take many many pictures of my gold. I show mother gold. I tell madam keep. I no go back, madam take all. Money madam also take.

'Madam, mother happy also sad I go home five days only. I cook chicken rice, *mee siam*[57], and satay. Nobody eat. Mother so sad. She ask what I eat in madam's house.

'Madam, mother say sister mother-in-law no already. They want sell land and house. House four rooms one bathroom. No tap, we take water from well no pay. Got tap pay money. Now we bathe in the house. Got electric, TV set. I send money buy house. Yes, Madam, my money in bank enough. No, I no go home, I money keep. I put house in brother name. Yes, madam, don worry, my brother very good, no take.'

So Kamani now had a piece of property, fully paid in cash, lived in by her brother and his family, rent free.

'Madam, see this picture in newspaper. This girl my friend Athula. We go out together. She go home already, work twelve years in Singapore. Newspaper say she buy wheelchair, new one give old people house. This Athula, this doctor, this old woman in her wheelchair. Athula say Singapore give very good money. Now she got house, money, some gold, her family happy, so she help old people. Wheelchair Singapore money $145. Madam, when I go home I give one wheelchair. I tell Buddha already.'

One evening Kamani surprised me. 'Madam, I want see your church.' From then on Kamani started her Catholic journey. She got a Sinhalese bible, and together we shared bible stories. She told me stories of her gods, how the gods created the earth, the

---

57 Spicy fried noodles.

sky, the sun, the moon, the people, animals and plants; how the gods protect as well as punish their peoples. Buddha is also very good. She concluded that Jesus is like Buddha and her gods.

'Madam, I want go school. My friend go school, learn sewing at church. $60 six months, one month two times, can?' Her new Singer sewing machine with a foot pedal was a proud neighbour of the piano. When Kamani was ready to go home, she was able to sew simple blouses and children's clothes. This new skill would bring in additional income.

Then, one day, Kamani revealed that she had been dating a very nice Indian man working as a gardener at the Botanic Gardens for the past two years. They planned to get married. However, her and his parents objected to the union. 'Madam, mother say, I cannot go Sri Lanka if I marry Indian man. His mother also say same. How, Madam?'

The testimonial got her a job in Cyprus. She was certain she would be employed by a 'good madam'. I always marvelled at foreign domestic help, most with minimal education, and little money on them, in debt, courageously marching into the world far removed from theirs, undaunted by the magnitude of the unknown, with perhaps only picture postcards of their intended destination, and with no support from the family. Kamani chose Cyprus.

'Agent say Cyprus boyfriend easy find job. Canada very far, very cold. My new madam Catholic, like madam. They know speak English. I go first boyfriend go later. He no get job yet.'

Cyprus welcomed her. Her new home was a property on the cliff by the sea. Cold winds embraced her. Her employer treated her well. She had her own little 'house', a five-minute walk from the main house. She was given woollies, coats, boots, a beanie and gloves and a walkie-talkie. Her diet changed completely, from steamed pork, tofu and curry to salads, breads, roasts and soups. Her weekly share of two bottles of wine – a white and a red – were politely returned. She was happy.

'Madam, this grandma just like madam's mother. So good, like friend, not maid. We go church every morning. Everybody surprise, say my English very good. Also new grandma ask where I learn about Jesus.

'Madam, happy birthday. Madam, I send madam four bottles wine, two red and two white. The wine here very nice.' 'Madam, Merry Christmas.' 'Madam, happy new year. When Chinese New Year? I not sure when, January or February. Calendar in Cyprus no Chinese New Year.

'No madam, one year already, boyfriend still no come. Said cannot get job. He ask me $2500, and I tell him I have no money, he very angry. He not call me. He not answer my calls. Better I stay and work here.

'Madam, I getting married. He Iranian, very, very good man. Yes, he Muslim. He supervisor transport-company, carry things from factory to shops. Mother? Mother say I nearly 40 years old. So better get married. We go pay respects to family, next month. Then we go to Iran. I become Muslim in Iran and we marry in his house. His parents agree. They see my photos and say they like me. We can live in Iran.

'Thank you madam, but please don't send gold. Registered post also no use. Only empty envelope I get. Money? No, please don't.

'Madam, I at airport now. When I marry I send you wedding photos and new telephone number. Thank you madam for everything.'

I did not receive any call, wedding photos or hear from Kamani again. My calls were unanswered, no such number. Kamani, my dear, dear Kamani, I think of you often. My friends who knew you also enquired. Where are you? How are you? No one knows. We pray for your well-being.

The Girl In The Taj Mahal

This story tells my experience as a lecturer during classroom observations of my trainees. The story is an accurate account of life in a rubber estate. Scholarships were offered to students who were accepted by the university. All workers always had a yearning to 'go home' to India one day to visit the Taj Mahal, when they had saved enough. Many others however chose to settle in their adopted country. My story revolves round this estate.

The gods were sad, and they wept. Or perhaps they were angry. No one knew for sure. And their tears formed waterfalls. But as there were no mountains or high ground in the rubber estate, their tears formed rivers, gushing muddy water uncontrollably into the estate. No one in the rubber estate community knew why this watery punishment was meted on them; they were convinced they had displeased the gods.

'Ritesh, ma! Ritesh, ma!' The mother, shaded under a banana leaf, stood outside the school and called out for her son. The teacher looked out the window and, competing with the sound and fury of the rain, shouted back, 'What do you want?'

'I give Ritesh banana leaf.'

'Which class?'

'Don't know.' Every day when it rained, mothers, shaded under a banana leaf umbrella, called out to their children to hand them a leaf umbrella.

Ritesh, his parents and grandparents and two brothers lived in a small rubber estate community. They had arrived in a small boat from India to this new country, Malaysia. The children were in school as the recruiting agent had promised.

The villagers were poor, uneducated, landless, greatly in debt, with several children to feed. Life was a struggle. The recruiting agent understood their struggles. He also understood Malaysia needed thousands of cheap labour to tap the rubber trees for latex, a major export. He relished his trips home to recruit young men to work in Malaysia. He was all smiles, seeing himself banking in his substantial recruiting agent fees. He was persuasive and had great emotional intelligence.

'*Annan*[58], here no work, no land, no money. I take you work in Malaysia. Big rubber estate. Got plenty job, tap rubber. There good. Every worker get one house, got two rooms. Got land. Can plant vegetables, get some chickens. You work get plenty money, can buy goat, cow also can. Get milk, sell get more money.'

The villagers were confused. Many questions and fears were raised. 'Where this country? How go? Who people work there? What rubber? Never see. How work there? What we eat? Got dhal? Got tomatoes? How cut tree and tree not die. We cut tree

---

58 Brother.

make fire, cook food. Got people speak Tamil?'

Their questions answered, fears of this new land diminished. 'The *mandor* teach you how work. He supervisor very good man.' The villagers were interested. Then in subdued tones, the prize catch, the bait he knew would trap the villagers. 'In Malaysia, all children must go school. Children no go school, *appa* and *am'ma* police catch go jail.'

Ritesh's family, like many others, had dreamed of the brilliant future their children would have as doctors, teachers and perhaps even becoming a minister in their home village. They hugged their carpetbags and set sail in a small, overcrowded, probably unseaworthy, boat to this new land of great promises.

In their new home in a rubber estate in the state of Pahang, parents and grandparents were grateful they had a job tapping rubber. They also had a small house with two rooms, a sitting room and a shared kitchen with another family, and land around the house where they could plant vegetables. And the good agent was right, their only son and grandson, Ritesh, was in the estate school. They were happy. Their two older children had died of disease. They did not know what the disease was; the doctor had said it was a bad disease, the hospital was far away, they had no money. The *mandor* explained, 'The company has no money for medicine. Money for medicine is only for workers; the boys are not workers.' The supervisor gave them some money from the company. So they buried the two boys, and moved to this new community somewhere in Johore, hoping for a new life for their only remaining child, Ritesh.

Ritesh was six years old and placed in Primary 1. He spoke his mother tongue at home. In school he learnt a little English and his lessons were in Bahasa, the national language and medium of instruction in Malaysia. Soon he was able to write his name in the English alphabet, R-i-t-e-s-h. He was a good student. His parents and grandparents drilled into him, 'Ritesh, very important go school and learn all lessons. Then you become very clever. No need to wake up 3 morning tap rubber. You become doctor or teacher or minister and become rich.' Ritesh etched all these in his heart.

Two years later a new *guru besar*, the headteacher, arrived with his wife and his daughter. Ritesh had never seen a more beautiful girl. Unfortunately she was a baby. Nonetheless, he decided that when he grew up he would marry her, and be a headmaster too, and they would live happily ever after, just like in the movies. But he had watched only one movie in his eight years. It was Deepavali and the estate manager had screened the movie in his garden for all the staff. The movie was screened five times. Ritesh watched it five times like everyone else.

Ritesh couldn't remember the title, nor the story, nor the actors and actresses, nor the songs, but he remembered them as the most melodious songs he had ever heard, and the most graceful dances he had ever watched. Most of all he remembered the girl. The girl with the most beautiful face, the most beautiful long, shiny black hair flowing down to her waist as she danced, the most beautiful eyes, the most beautiful lips, the most beautiful voice and the most beautiful name. She was dancing and singing around the most beautiful building in the world, the Taj Mahal.

After the movie he asked his grandfather, '*Daa-daa-jee*, what is the Taj Mahal?'

Daa-daa-jee spoke Tamil, fearful his grandson might forget his mother tongue. 'It is the most beautiful building in the world. It is very large, very, very large. There are many rooms inside. If you sleep only one night in one room from the day you were born, you will be twenty-five years old when you complete sleeping in all the rooms. The walls are white, and many workers must clean them every day. Taj Mahal is a holy place. Their great ruler built for wife because he loved her very much.'

'What is his name daa-daa-jee?'

Daa-daa-jee explained he was a great shah but forgot his name. 'It is a beautiful palace, with water round it; fish swim in it and other animals also live in the gardens. It is so beautiful that animals do not fight; lions and deer eat grass together; snakes can carry rats on their long backs to wherever the rats want to go; white horses marry black horses and their children got black and white stripes. Before I die I want to visit the Taj Mahal. Ritesh, you study hard and become clever boy, and become rich, and take me there.'

Ritesh promised his grandfather. That night he wrote in his English reader, '*I will study hard to be clever. I want to be an airline pilot and take my daa-daa-jee to the Taj Mahal.*' A few days later he added '*my maa-maa-jee, appa and am'ma also.*' And another few days later, '*and the girl in the Taj Mahal.*' He thought it only right that as he wanted to be a clever boy and become an airline pilot, he should write completely in English, every word.

To grandfather, father and Ritesh, the Taj Mahal *is* the Taj

Mahal, never Taj or Mahal. That would be most disrespectful to this great and majestic palace of the great shah. They did not know his name. They only knew he was a great shah.

Daa-daa-jee told him many stories about the Taj Mahal. It took 20,000 artisans to build it. It took fifty years to build it. The white stones came from around the world, some from faraway China, some from faraway India.

'Daa-daa-jee Taj Mahal is in India.'

'India is very big. Some stones came from England. The king of England heard about this beautiful palace and gave some stones.'

'The king of England also knew about the Taj Mahal?'

'Of course, all kings in Europe heard about this beautiful palace.'

'Did they come to see it?'

'Not yet, not ready. On nights when the moon is round and bright and no wind, you can see two Taj Mahal, one white in the moonlight and one black in the water.'

And every story grandfather told him added on to its beauty and splendour and the girl in the Taj Mahal. Lying in bed, Ritesh saw himself weaving among the banana plants, the papaya plants, the rambutan trees, the mango trees and the rubber trees. He removed the hard shells of the rubber seeds and used them as fish bait. He put the seeds inside the *bubu* and the aromatic smell of the seeds attracted the fish into the trap. Once, he caught 37 fish in his *bubu*. He gave them all to the girl in the Taj Mahal. She was about to hug him, when one of the fish nibbled on his finger and he woke up. He sobbed for lost love.

And for several years Ritesh dreamed of the girl in the Taj Mahal. He knew everything about her. They talked for hours, danced and sang round the gardens, weaved their way around the papaya and banana plants, the rambutan and rubber tress. They were happy.

When the new headmaster arrived with his wife and Aasha his daughter, Ritesh knew his girl in the Taj Mahal had arrived Aasha was in Primary 1, Ritesh was in Primary 4.

On their first rainy day Ritesh shared his leaf umbrella with Aasha, his girl in the Taj Mahal, but she had a real umbrella. That night Ritesh said to his mother, 'Am'ma, the guru besar says mothers cannot shout for their children outside the school. It is very rude.'

'You bring banana leaf to school.'

'No one can cut a banana leaf. The guru besar explained if everyone did that there would be no leaves on banana plants, then there would be no more banana plants. And no more bananas. If I bring one, I cannot go to school anymore.' No mothers ever again took refuge under a banana leaf umbrella.

The guru besar's daughter had a pencil box and coloured pencils. She was also very clever. She could sing 'Miss Polly Has a Dolly', 'Sing a Song of Six Pence', 'Ding Dong Bell' and many other strange songs. Ritesh learnt these songs as he was determined he would be worthy of her. He carried her bag to her house, exactly eleven steps away from his family's room. He picked flowers for her hair, caught spiders for her, but no, she didn't like spiders. So Ritesh no longer liked spiders. All the children played with rubber seeds that were plentiful. They played 'who can collect the most seeds to the count of twenty'. The girl in the Taj Mahal did not like to lose, so Ritesh made sure she never lost. They discovered that rubbing two seeds together or against a hard surface, made the seeds hot. Ah the greatest fun – *chap* your unsuspecting friend, the prized place was on the cheek. One had to be stealthy to achieve that. The girl in the Taj Mahal cried when she was *chap-ed*, so Ritesh always received the *chap*, twice over. They played *guli* with the seeds. It did not matter when the seed marbles were lost. There were countless more. When the rains came and the *parits* overflowed, they caught little fish and kept them in little jars. When it no longer rained and the streams were a trickle, they forgot the fish, until the next rainy season.

Later that year the rubber plantation was sold to another large international company. The new management offered scholarships to all children who completed their primary school and passed all the exams to continue secondary school in the nearest town. Ritesh remembered his promise to daa-daa-jee and studied very hard under the light of the kerosene lamp, which hung on the wall by the kitchen. On windy nights, the swinging lamp created strange shadows on the wall, but all Ritesh saw was the girl in the Taj Mahal happily dancing, just for him. He felt sad when the oil flickered its last breath of life, and his homework was still not completed. Grandfather smoked much less, and toddy was not seen again. The wick in the oil lamp stayed awake much longer.

When the time came for Ritesh to leave for the town school, he promised the girl in the Taj Mahal he would write to her every day. He did not promise his daa-daa-jee because no one in his family could read. The first month Ritesh found everything strange and he fell sick. Then he remembered his promise to daa-daa-jee and miraculously recovered. He wanted to tell the girl in the Taj Mahal everything about the new school and the new town; students did not go home during recess, they bought food from the tuck shop; he did not know what foods they were, never seen them and he was sick; around the town where there were endless streams of cars but no cows or goats; you had to buy bananas and papayas and coconuts, not pluck them off the trees. If you did that, the police would catch you and you would be sent to jail. But there were no such plants in the town. He didn't write because he couldn't. He didn't have money for 'letter' paper, envelopes and the 8-cent stamps. But the main reason he didn't write was he did not know the address. No one in the estate had ever received a letter. The *mandor* told the community everything they needed to know. No one asked, nor questioned; everyone listened, believed and accepted whatever the estate supervisor told them. Everyone was content with life.

During the long year-end holidays, Ritesh went home. He had missed all the excitement of what had happened in the community. Two years into secondary school, one November-December holiday, Ritesh found himself in a new community. All the old houses were gone. There were new living quarters, and each family had more rooms. Ritesh now had his own room. He cherished that, enjoying his privacy. But at times alone in the dark, enveloped in his private thoughts, he missed the stale yet still sweet fragrance of maa-maa-jee's jasmine or frangipani flowers in her hair, and daa-daa-jee's stale tobacco and toddy smell when he slept between them. He could not find his English reader where he had written 'I will study hard to be clever. I want to be an airline pilot and take my grandfather to the Taj Mahal,', 'my grandmother, and father and mother also', 'and the girl in the Taj Mahal'. But he remembered – it was buried in his heart. One does not forget one's name – Ritesh, lord of truth.

'Daa-daa-jee, what happened?'

Daa-daa-jee told him. One morning when they were preparing to go to the trees, a kerosene lamp overturned and a fire started. It spread so quickly and burnt most of the twenty-over-years-old attap and wooden houses. It was good there were no doors to any of the houses, so people were able to run out quickly.

'Were you hurt?'

'No one was hurt. The manager asked whose kerosene lamp it was.'

'Whose was it?'

'Everyone said, "Don't know!" I told the manager, "Why you ask stupid question? Already burnt everything. You must help us build new houses and buy clothes. See my pots and plates here? All black and broken!!! And my wife and I have no clothes! You want all the people here to be naked or what!" Everyone clapped their hands. I was a hero. I was very happy.'

Daa-daa-jee told him every detail, as he did with the Taj Mahal, as he always did with every story about Mother India. The monsoons had come early. They were not prepared. The winds and the rains were like Kunchikal Falls not resting even for one minute! The winds were hurricanes, howling loudly like many mad people running from everywhere to nowhere. The water and the wind were competing to see which was the stronger. So much water and wind just like when they were in the boat on their way over from India. The roofs leaked, some caved in, some were blown off; vegetables drowned; many of the chickens were blown away; cows became sick and there was no milk. Two goats died. Everyone was very scared. Even the Manager was scared. He came with the mandor and spoke to them and promised to help them. There was no tapping to do. The rule said, 'No work, no pay.'

'Maybe Lord Siva is angry.'

Daa-daa-jee concluded sternly, 'Let's not talk about Lord Siva. He's our God, and he must have his reasons. Maybe we were bad.'

'Daa-daa-jee what did you do to find food?'

'The manager is a good man. He gave every family ten kilos of rice, two kilos sugar, salt, seven big packets of dhal and curry powder, ten tins of Milkmaid condensed milk and two dozen cans of Yeo Hiap Seng chicken curry. Three days later when the mandor told him many old people were sick, he gave every daa-daa-jee and daa-dee-maa two bottles of Brands Essence Of Chicken. I like it, tastes a little like toddy. Maa-maa-jee did not like it. Am'ma drank hers. I and appa like it. There was enough food for everyone. The mandor is a good man. He gave every worker exactly what the manager said to give. But his understanding of food distribution for children and people who are not tappers is not very good.'

The community prayed to Ganesha. When the sun mopped up the water, the opposite happened. Everything became tinder dry. They had prayed too hard for dry weather. But then again Ganesha is a good god. The fire was good. It gave them new houses with asbestos roofs, with doors and a latch, and more rooms for each family. The year was a good year even though they lived amidst the rubble for about six months.

'So you see, Ritesh, everything happens for a reason. You must always remember to pray. Doors are not necessary, what have we got that thieves want? There are no thieves here. Everyone good.'

'In my school, all doors have locks. Even the desks have locks. And in the classrooms, the teacher switches on the fan from 10 o'clock until school finishes at 1.15. There is one fan in the middle of the ceiling. So nice.'

'A fan? Why do you need a fan? The trees give us wind. So nice here.'

The manager had installed two large generators and every house had electricity from 3 to 6.30 in the morning. The tappers could see clearly when they collected their equipment and got ready for work – no more risk of fires. And lights on again from 6 to 10 in the evening. The manager said this would help students study. As a Deepavali present, he gave every family a Philips portable radio with six AAA batteries. The mandor and the manager's driver were very clever. Now the radios could run on electricity from the generator. The music blasting from all houses tuning in to the same station in the mornings and evenings reverberated through the trees. Ritesh was again darting between the rubber trees and rambutan trees and banana plants with the girl in the Taj Mahal.

Daa-daa-jee said, 'This is good. The gods know we are happy.

The manager knows about the radios. He is also happy as he never complained. We think he likes our music. The manager's house has electricity all day.' The manager's 'big house' was a 20-minute drive away. One day daa-daa-jee suggested to Ritesh, 'after you has become a clever boy, you can also work as a manager and everybody will have electricity all day.' Ritesh was set on being an airline pilot.

Ritesh did well in his secondary school. The company paid for his university studies. He became a mechanical engineer, the first graduate from his community. The whole estate celebrated. The manager donated three goats and one hundred bottles of FnN Orange and Sarsi drinks. They had rainbow jellies, Cadbury chocolates with nuts and raisins, but the greatest treat was the Magnolia cup ice cream that came with little splinter paddle spoons. The manager had kept the ice cream in an ice cream cooler in his house until the end, when he and his driver proudly honked their way in. That was the epitome of honour for Ritesh and the community. He made a short speech that the mandor translated: 'Dear Ritesh, our company is most proud of you. You have brought great honour to your parents, to the community and to the company. You are a model for other children here. Encourage them to study hard and go to university, like you. And for you, please say a few words to your family and community that had supported you. Also what your plans are. Finally, to get you started in your new life, this is a briefcase for you with your name, the name of this estate and today's date. Always remember your roots.' The applause was like the thunderous Kunchikal Falls. The gods were smiling down on them.

Ritesh was both gratified and humbled. He replied in English so the manager could understand. The mandor again did the translation: 'Thank you very much from the bottom of my heart, Mr Manager, for the scholarship. I never thought I could achieve this. It is through the unconditional love of my family and community and unfailing faith of the company of my abilities that I have succeeded. I want to be an airline pilot so that I can take my grandfather, father and mother to see the Taj Mahal. That is my only wish. I love you all.' The celebrations continued well after lights out.

Ritesh wanted a job in an airline company. A promise to daa-daa-jee is a promise. He had to hurry. The promise to maa-maa-jee was lost. When he was finally able to, he took daa-daa-jee to the Taj Mahal. Grandfather was a ten-year-old Ritesh, listening to the wonderful stories of the Taj Mahal: the waters, the trees, every detail. He saw in his mind's eye the lions and the deer eating grass together, the snakes carrying the rats, the children of the white and black horses, catching fish in the water, caressing the seeds of rubber trees he loved so much. 'Ritesh, did you bring the bubu? And the rubber seeds? How many fish did you catch? 37! That's good, we cook them tonight. Ritesh are there any ripe bananas? Please pluck one for me.' Grandfather was happy, Ritesh was happy. Ritesh finally found his girl in the Taj Mahal. She was the Taj Mahal.

Lily

Decades ago the prejudice against intermarriage was generally one of race (among Chinese, Indians and Malays) and religion. Families have disowned their children. However, intermarriages with Caucasians were acceptable. This story is based on a personal family tragedy, fictionalised to protect the innocent and the guilty.

Lily lay in the hospital bed, her face pale, her pulse slow, her spirit waiting to leave. The doctors surrounded her, knowing the flat line was seeping its way in, but still trying their best to revive her when they knew they couldn't – and, now knowing what she had taken, they knew she wouldn't want them to.

'We had to pump her, to clean her. She took a lot – most of the pills had dissolved; but the liquids, three different ones, have gone through her system, burnt her organs. The next two days are crucial.' The doctors were sombre, 'Mr Low, Mrs Low, Lily slept to the end.'

Mrs Janice Low sobbed. Even her husband was not sure what or whom the tears were for. For a daughter, too young to give up her life? For the family, losing the only daughter and sister? For herself, a daughter who committed suicide would certainly raise questions from among her social circle 'Why? How? When? Where?' The shame she felt that Lily, her first born whom she had raised and loved and nurtured into a beautiful young woman, a most eligible professional woman, from a respectable family, had committed suicide would be most insufferable. If Lily died, how would she explain it, she had asked herself hundreds of times. Well, Lily enjoyed scuba diving, she drowned off the Great Barrier Reef; she fell off the horse on her first ride and broke her neck while on holiday in Mongolia; she suffered a ruptured appendix on an expedition through Patagonia and had to be flown home but it was too late, and several more options. Which of these would be most believable? How to flesh out the story?

Mr Henry Low intercepted her thoughts. 'Janice, why did it have to be this way?' Gentle in voice, he knew why, yet needed to ask the 'why' question. He felt guilty, regretted not expressing his feelings and right judgement, and was tormented with longing for a much-loved daughter. Lily had messaged him a day earlier, 'Daddy, my daddy, I love you so much. Hug William and Jamie and tell them I love them very much too. Tell Mother she wins.' He did not tell his wife. Mr Low had felt a sense of foreboding. His messages were not replied to. Calls not answered. He went to her flat, no lights on. Rang the bell. No door opened. Called for the locksmith. It had happened. Too late. Lily on the bed, pale, bottles of pills and liquids beside her.

He recalled with intense sorrow, the happy times he had shared with Lily. The times he carried her on his shoulders, and she had shrieked in delight, 'Daddy you're my pony. I can ride very fast, I'll never fall off.' The times he taught his three children to swim, from paddling in water to snorkelling. He remembered Lily's first boy interest. He had invited him to a movie, 'Indiana Jones', just the three of them. They had tea at Burger King. 'Lily, we'll go to Indiana Jones country and ride a horse very fast through the valley at Petra after your final exams, he had promised, and they did. The times he covered her eyes from the kissing scenes on TV. 'Too young to kiss!' he had said. And the time he watched over her two days and two nights when she had chickenpox. He moaned, 'Lily, I love you so much.'

Janice Low played detective in her mind, 'Who murdered Lily?' The family relationship came apart when 'that person', Cyril Puticheri, Lily's chosen life partner came into the picture. Mr Low approved of Cyril, liked the young man for his sense of humour, and his love for Lily.

After Lily's private funeral, Mrs Janice Low had sent her maid to ask 'that person's' parents to return the key to her daughter's HDB[59] flat, to 'get my daughter's things'. Janice found the flat pathetic. Cheap local furniture and furnishings. Only one bedroom furnished. Kitchen nothing much. In the pantry some instant noodles, breakfast foods, and beverages. She screamed, how could anyone start married life and be happy living there? She wept for her daughter's unhappiness.

On the dressing table was Lily's journal. It stunned her to read Lily's thoughts and feelings.

* * *

59 Housing and Development Board, a government project for public housing in Singapore.

3 February

Dear Dairy, I need to pen my thoughts and feelings. Cyril takes Mother so lightly, brushing her off, no relevance in our lives. He's probably right.

I pleaded. Mother, why could you not accept Cyril? It is laughable that Mother could say I will be eating curry and chapatti every meal, and I would become dhal[60]! She is a racist, calling the children we would have, 'kopi susu[61]' with unpronounceable names. Several times daddy had tea with Cyril at Komala's restaurant at Serangoon. Cyril told us funny stories about himself and his family. Daddy, you accept Cyril. Can't you reason with Mother? I know you want to keep the peace, as you so often say. You feel intimidated, aware that you achieved social status when you married Mother. And Mother never stops reminding you, your Hugo Boss suits, LV shoes and all that. Daddy, I sense you felt trapped. So you know how trapped I feel. Daddy, my daddy, could you, would you talk to Mother? Please.

* * *

'Janice, I would like a quiet time with you after dinner, please.'
'What about?'
'Lily and Cyril.'
'There's nothing to talk!'
'We must. Please.'
We did talk. What devil had got into Henry to invite 'that

---

60 Lentils, preferred by Indians as curry.
61 Coffee with milk, a derogatory term for children of mixed Chinese and Indian heritage.

*person' into my house! How could he ever understand 'that
person' could never be part of my family? His family must have
put in something in his food or drink to get him so compliant.
Why did he spend time with them? We fought. Surprised Henry
would fight me! As always, he was lost for words. Meek as a
mouse. I brought him into society, the golf, the private clubs.*

* * *

10 March
This evening we asked for your blessings to marry, you wept
openly, you wept for yourself. You felt shame that I wished to
marry 'that person'. 'That person' has a name, Mother. Cyril
Puticheri. Cyril, my classmate is a responsible, loving man. A
lawyer like us. Yes, we live in a 'good class bungalow', play golf,
we go on annual holidays abroad. Yes, Cyril grew up in a four-
room HDB flat, has two older married sisters. So what!!!

His dad is, in your eyes, 'only a primary school teacher, did
not even step into university', and his mum, 'What! Part-time
child minder?' Mother, you don't understand. They are humble,
beautiful-in-the-soul people. There is much pride in what they do,
what they have, what they have achieved. They are happy. They
accept me and love me. And YES! YES! YES! Mother, Cyril and I
are happy in our five-room HDB flat in Sengkang!

Daddy, when we told you we were getting married, you
hugged me so tightly, I almost couldn't breathe. You wouldn't
let me go. You clasped Cyril's hands in yours, then patted him on
both shoulders. You said *'Take good care of Lily'* and I read in

your eyes what you had so often said to me, '*Any guy who breaks your heart, I'll break his neck.*' I told Cyril that. He laughed and said you are a funny guy. Daddy, I love you.

* * *

Lily, you have shattered my heart, destroyed my family. I cried for you, what would happen to you? Why ask for my blessing when you were already adamant about getting married? Didn't you realise family ties are a priority to get on in this world? Be somebody. With 'that person' you could never be. Just like your Yeh Yeh – a nobody! A nobody! And the smell of the ... of that family! Lily, I wanted you to be happy. How could you be happy in an HDB flat? And the housework. You don't even know how to boil an egg. Or load a washing machine. No maid to clean and cook for you. No Jacuzzi to relax in. I raised you into a perfect image of me, well groomed, right society. Wait till his family bullies you, then don't come running to me! Your father! A weakling, a mouse, no opinion to stand on. You twisted him round your little finger.

I couldn't sleep that night. Henry was reading. Reading 1984! Said he wanted to study the ways of Big Brother. That crap book! I wanted to smash it in his face. We are a democracy, a family and we discuss what is best for our family. By extension, we contribute all our good genes. Peter, Minister's only child is so madly in love with you Lily. His parents really wanted you as a daughter-in-law. Lily, a minister's daughter-in-law! What could be more perfect? Now you've lost him.

* * *

2 May

Cyril and his parents advised us to get Mother's blessing, whatever it takes. This morning I asked Mother to plan our wedding with us. She said she was planning on a Mediterranean cruise. I wished her an enjoyable cruise.

She lambasted me for being an ingrate; said she had provided me with all that I wanted, above all that I needed. What would our relatives say? If he's a white man, yes, that's perfectly acceptable. But an Indian! Living in an HDB flat in Jurong? And his family? A school teacher, a part-time child minder, a secondary school teacher daughter, ok a graduate; a social worker second daughter, ok also a graduate. What status is there in social work? And also, they are Christians! 'That person' as the only son would have to give most of his salary to them! What is left would not be enough for a Prada wallet at the Salvation Army Thrift Shop! She demanded an answer, what kind of a life is that? I told her it would be a wonderful life of love and simplicity, no pretences and plenty of time to smell the flowers. She was on the verge of slapping me.

Daddy interrupted us. '*Lily, you give up Cyril, I'll never talk to you again.*' Mother screamed all the profanities at Daddy, reminding him he was NOTHING until he married her. Furious, he stomped out of the house, William and Jamie followed him. They were 'lost' till the next evening. No, wouldn't tell where they were. I knew, at Nai-Nai[62] and Ye-Ye, daddy's parents.

We had a BIG fight. I accused Mother of being money face, which is absolutely true!

---

62 Father's mother. Ye-Ye is father's dad.

'The best gift for Mummy is to give up 'that person'. I love you so much. Give up that person and all will be good. I promise.'

'If I don't?'

'You'll be sorry. You lose everything, everything means everything. That also means me. I will die of shame, nowhere to put my face. You want mother to die?'

'No, Mother, you won't die. I don't want you to die.' Death is probably afraid of Mother.

'Mother, do you love Daddy? Really, really love him as a man, a husband, a lover, a father? Mother can you tell me what is love?' She never answered. She loves no one, not even herself!

* * *

Prepare for her wedding? What wedding? I will not be part of it. Never! I could see unhappiness written on their faces, oozing out of everywhere. Henry, why did we get married? We were classmates. You were smart, on scholarship, top the class. Of course I had to have you, only the top student for me. You were the most handsome man, the most serene, regal, unassuming. You wanted my social status. I believed we would be a perfect pair, though my parents were not quite so happy. We educated you into society. I was resplendent in my Prada wedding gown. You enjoyed the grooming, the private clubs, holidays abroad all of which you never had till you married me! Your father had to borrow a suit for our wedding! My parents paid for that dinner! Are you a good father? Yes, I suppose. As a husband? Yes, always obliging me. As a lover? We have three children.

* * *

4 July
I'm looking at my favourite photo of Nai-Nai and Ye-Ye eating at the market stalls. They reminded me not to tell Mother we ate at the hawker centre. We could only eat at restaurants and the club cafés. Several times Daddy took us and Ye-Ye and Nai-Nai to various stalls.

* * *

So, they conspired behind my back ... those ... people. Sneaking out to be with them. Henry you cheated on me, you unfaithful man! Now I know why Jamie coughs often – the dirty market stalls! And Lily, I understand now it blasted your brains into wanting to marry 'that person'. Well, the accident was his karma, seducing my Lily for her status.

* * *

28 July
Nai-Nai passed away today. She suffered a heart attack, alone at home. I lost my Nai-Nai, the best grandma in the world. I know you are with Jesus, even though you are a Buddhist.

Ye-Ye lost his wife, his confidante, his best friend. He will never be his laughing self again. He may lose the will to live. He will only wait for Nai-Nai to invite him to join her. Cyril and I will spend every Sunday with him.

* * *

Lily, you chose to spend time with them instead of shopping with me?

* * *

3 November

This morning Ye-Ye passed away in the hospital. He fell off his bicycle, hit his head on the curb. The hospital called Daddy and he called me. Cyril and I arrived first. Ye-Ye waited for Daddy, Jamie and William. His firm grip told us he loved us very much. He smiled, let go of our hands and closed his eyes.

* * *

They had their lives. They lived the way they wanted. They were never kind to me, not really accepting me into the family. If I had been there, he would have refused to hold my hand.

* * *

6 November

This morning we went to Bright Hill Columbarium. Daddy placed Nai-Nai's and Ye-Ye's urns in the niche, together in life, together in death. Daddy was sombre. He clasped my hand, we shared the same thoughts; words were not necessary. William and Jamie sobbed uncontrollably, clinging on to Daddy and me. Cyril had arms long enough to embrace all of us. Mother had a headache and couldn't come.

* * *

Only I am brave enough to tell the truth. They are in a better place.

* * *

18 December

We received the keys to our HDB apartment five months ago. We have furnished it, and I decided to move out to our new home, Cyril's and mine. Daddy hugged and kissed me and said, '*I love you girl, I love you very much. Be happy.*' He gave me a heart-shaped gold pendent with a simple inscription, 'I LOVE YOU', and the look in his eyes said the unsaid, Mother need not know. Daddy and Cyril loaded my things into their cars and with J and W we drove to our apartment. We had a great time advising one another what to put where. We had family bonding. William and Jamie called Cyril 'bro'. Cyril's parents invited us for lunch. We were so happy. Mother said she had a facial appointment that day.

* * *

So you chose to cohabit. Have you no dignity, Lily? Henry, I'm disappointed. You cheated on me again! Like your parents, stabbed me in the back. A plain gold pendent! Cheapskate. I have my complete set of ruby and emeralds and jade.

31 December

We invited Daddy, Mother, Jamie and William over for a New Year's Eve dinner. Daddy SMSed me: *Darling, Law Society Annual Dinner. Apologies. Love lots always. I'll call you.* Mother made that decision. To be seen at the 'right place', on the 'right occasion' with the 'right people', in the 'right attire' was paramount, nothing else mattered.

We had a celebration with Cyril's family. There was a great deal of noise, yet a deafening silence, an emptiness in my heart. Cyril noticed, told him we would not spoil our family's happiness.

* * *

Lily Lily what have done to destroy your future.

* * *

1 January

I cried the whole of last night. Asked for time alone to collect my thoughts. Friends told me that parents' objection to their children's marriage for whatever reason was temporary. When the grandchildren arrive, joy and love return. They don't know Mother. I need to talk to Daddy, my Daddy. Daddy, we know you came from a humble family. Being the youngest of three children you were fortunate that Aunty Amy and Aunty Rose were able to assist you in your uni days, even though you were on scholarship.

* * *

You were on scholarship, Henry, only some! You owed no one except me! I was your driver in my white Honda round campus, invited you to nice cafés for meals, not canteen fare, watched movies and bought you your required reading books.

* * *

14 January

This morning I went to get my wedding saris. Nai-Nai, if only you were here, you would be with me helping me with my wedding trousseau. You would be so happy to help me. You would insist on the reddest lipstick! Yes, Nai-Nai, I have the reddest lipstick. When I was a little girl you would dab a little perfume on my forehead, smell me, hug me then pat my bottom.

Will Daddy and Mother and Jamie and William be present? Sighhhhh. Daddy, I know you can't do anything against Mother, but surely you can say something? Daddy, please come, please Daddy and Jamie and William too. Just this once I'm pleading and begging, Daddy. Daddy SMS'd me: *Lily I will 'give you away' to Cyril. You deserve each other. William and Jamie excited – not attended a church wedding before.* Daddy, my Daddy and my William and Jamie. Love you lots, lots. Mother? Sighhhhhh.

* * *

We are not Christians. You could have had your Prada wedding gown. You would look resplendent as I was on my wedding day. Henry had decided to 'give away the bride' in the Christian wedding tradition. Give her away, done! Henry, William and Jamie are mine!

* * *

31 January

Nai-Nai, Ye-Ye, two days before my wedding Cyril died. He was on his way to church to finalise the wedding preparations and he was in a hit and run accident. He had borrowed a friend's motorbike, as our car was being decorated for the wedding. Cyril was declared 'deceased' when I arrived at the hospital.

I called home and Mother answered, 'Mother, Cyril died in a hit and run accident this morning.' And what was her response? She sounded relieved, telling me, 'Now you're free, my darling. We're back as a family. First things first. We go collect your things from there. Then we need to go to HDB to settle that place. It now belongs to you. I'll check whether you can sell it, or we have to return it to HDB. Then the car has to be sold ...' I did not wish to listen to her long tirades. I could not understand how a mother could be so soulless, so cruel, so punishing to her own daughter. Mother, you just plunged your lifetime warranty Senshi knife into me. No, knives don't kill. People kill. Mother you win. I let you win.

* * *

Janice Low convinced herself Lily was out of her mind, could not think straight. She was a good wife and mother, caring, loving.

Must be 'that person' who turned her against the family. She wept as befitting a mother who had to bury her child. Henry was too weak, weeping like a baby. He walked out on the family after the funeral. William and Jamie went with him. They abandoned me. He should be clearing this matter. I have to do all this! No one cared for me.

She must remain strong. Tomorrow she would hunt them down. She would find them easily, as she always had whenever Henry walked out. She wished Henry would verbally or even physically fight her. She would like a good fight and to win. No one must ever know of Lily's Journal. She decided that the best place for the journal was in a tub of water and bleach, then dump the papier-mâché into the rubbish bin the next day. Now, what would she tell her family, her friends, her colleagues? She couldn't think now, she was too tired. So many things to do tomorrow. She remembered Scarlet O'Hara's 'Tomorrow is another day'. Yes, tomorrow is another day. Tomorrow she would know what story to craft.

Kam Jian Ding, PhD

This is the story of a former colleague, a shy gentleman who was besotted with a young, enthusiastic female colleague, several years his junior. He may have possessed a high IQ but the same cannot be said of his EQ.

Kam Jiān Dìng, PhD, newly graduated from The University of North Carolina, USA, arrives at School of Education, Singapore University for the Arts, for his first day of the academic year to meet colleagues and staff before classes commence. He is thirty-three, of medium height, lank, and straight haired, with a mouth that does not seem to know there is such a thing as a smile. When he walks, he appears like a cut-out figure of a shorter Confucius *sans* beard.

Kam, PhD believes that in the sphere of education it is a requisite to put on a stern facial solemnity, thus portraying a well-educated educator. He is determined in educating his class to perfection.

At the first staff meeting, the dean invites new staff to self-introduce.

'Kam Jiān Dìng, PhD Philosophy, The University of North Carolina, major in Philosophy in Curriculum and Instruction

(Early Childhood Education). I completed my research in thirty months, the shortest time in the history of the university, according to my professors. The only objective of education is learning, not teaching. I have prepared a short sketch of learning and teaching.

'Here is Tan telling his friend Edwin he taught his dog Sterling to whistle. After a while Edwin says "I don't hear Sterling whistle" to which Tan replies "I said I taught him, I did not say he has learnt". Isn't that what educators have been doing, teaching and not caring whether learning has taken place? I believe Bloom's *Taxonomy of Educational Objectives* is the basis of sound education. Let me explain Bloom.'

The dean has to interrupt Kam, PhD. There are nine new staff. Kam loses his protest, is dejected but assures the staff he will expound Bloom further. He forgets Bloom was published in the 1950s. To regain his composure and perhaps his sense of superiority, he requests staff with PhDs raise their hands. No hands are raised and he curves his lips up into a satisfying smirk, unaware all present refuse to raise theirs.

Dr Kam enters Lecture Theatre 12 for his first lecture. He sees eager eyes focus on him and is pleased. 'Good morning, Ladies and Gentlemen, I am Dr Kam Jiān Dìng, PhD Philosophy, The University of North Carolina. My major is Philosophy in Curriculum and Instruction (Early Childhood Education). My research was completed in thirty months, the shortest time in the history of the university, according to my professors. The only objective of education is learning, not teaching. I have prepared a short sketch of learning and teaching. Here is Tan telling his friend Edwin he taught his dog Sterling to whistle. After a while Edwin says "I don't hear Sterling whistle" to which Tan replies "I said I taught him, I did not say he has learnt". Isn't that what educators have been doing, teaching and not caring whether learning has taken place? It is easy to teach, to ensure learning is difficult. But I am here to ensure learning. I always address my students "Ladies and Gentlemen" as respect is reciprocated with respect. You may address me "Doc",'

Bloom's taxonomy flashes on the screen, colourfully illustrated. The ladies and gentlemen's boredom is lost on Doc. He congratulates himself on captivating his audience. The semester goes much too fast for him. He has not demonstrated the applications of each of the subcategories of the learning domains in depth. He makes a pledge he will insist on extra classes. He is self-sacrificing for the good of future generations. It is his fiduciary duty.

Doc hardly chats with colleagues in the staff room. No time for idle chatter, he mummers. At the end of semester tea, he chooses to sit in a corner, feeds his belly with food and blooms his mind – there can never be enough of Bloom. Suddenly he yells excitedly, 'Yes, yes, yes!' closes his book, dismisses his plate, and skedaddles out. No one knows what the 'Yes, yes, yes!' is.

Doc sacrifices his vacation, scheming on how to get his ladies and gentlemen to debate him and the clever presentations of his subject. When the new semester starts Doc comes in as quietly as the falling leaves, several USBs on colourful lanyards strung round his neck like an overdressed mannequin displaying cheap accessories.

At his tutorial he is confident the debate, discussion and

learning will be PhD worthy. On the screen:

You have a class of fifteen five-year old children, twelve girls and three boys. The girls form cliques, refuse to play with the boys. The boys then form their group and display disruptive behaviour. How would you apply the Psychology of Learning to promote class cohesiveness?

The ladies and gentlemen squirm a great deal, study the doodles on their desks, and add several more. Doc is delighted his students are deep in thought, after all his purpose in life is to get students to think deeply. Finally a lady responds, 'Doc, small group discussion is of greater benefit then individual presentations. We have learned from you to think, analyse, discuss. When we discuss, two ideas from each grow into eight or more in a group.'

Doc agrees. He congratulates himself on having succeeded in teaching them independent learning.

Doc has to submit himself to a Class Lesson Observation, a requirement for confirmation into academia. Doc, with the cooperation of his ladies and gentlemen, delivers a lively discussion on the application of Bloom's *Domain on Psychomotor: Manual Skills Among Young Children.*

Invigorated and confirmed into academia, he is determined to show his charms. He surprises colleagues with greetings and smiles and even eats with them during lunch. That generates conjectures of female companions, a great inheritance or a 'born again' conversion. The semester over, several of Doc's colleagues conclude he is an amicable man after all, perhaps naïve in experiences of the ways of the world, or that he is simply unnecessarily worried about confirmation. Doc also pleads to be simply, 'Kam, just Kam, my friend'.

At the new semester two new staff self-introduce. Doc is now Kam, single and available. That generates agitated whispers that Doc is finally opening up and that is good. He remembers the conversation with Mother when he showed her his newly purchased bubble glass and a goldfish to put on his bedside table. She had told him quietly, 'You are thirty-three. Sleep with a woman, not a fish.'

Up she stands amongst them, 'Melissa Goh Kuà Lè, PhD, Adult Education, University of Otago at Dunedin, New Zealand, single and available, just.' When Kam meets the PhD eyes of Melissa he sojourns into the wild woods, into the rustic world of drifting yellow, brown, orange leaves, and the mating dance of the birds of paradise. The introduction of Dr Charles Apera Kingston from the same University of Otaga is only a murmuring in the breeze while Kam prances with Melissa in the woods.

'Welcome everyone, now let's have tea,' the dean announces.

'Electrifying lady, eh?' Mrs Ng comments. Kam smiles. He is scarlet with excitement and with some touch of embarrassment as he gingerly meanders among the staff and totters towards Melissa. She, amused by his awkward attempts at gaiety and contrived elegance, puts him at ease with, 'Kam, darling, what about dinner sometime. My place or yours?'

Scandalized at her public airing of great boldness at their first meeting, aware of the pricked eyes and ears in cemetery silence, he stammers, 'Yes, sure. We can go to Kopitiam across the road. The *nasi Padang*[63] there is good. The fish head ...'

---

63 Smorgasbord of Indonesian dishes.

'Kam darling, a vodka, Ritz Carlton. Then oysters or lobsters, and perhaps some dancing later?'

'I don't drink, I mean Mother doesn't like … I mean I can drink a little … shandy … you know some beer, some 7Up … maybe …'

'Kam, darling, I'll drink my vodka, then I'll drink yours, mummy darling wouldn't know.'

She is amused by his solemn air and puckered mouth, and sets him down as a mummy's boy, to be taught to be a man. She can't help becoming curious about this single and available man. Melissa explains she had said 'dinner sometime', that is, in the future, and the fish head and the vodka have to wait.

During the semester, Kam believes Melissa's daily bold 'darling' is for him and the occasional soft 'darling' to others are a modest distraction of her interest in him. Kam, besotted with Melissa, only feels the innumerable strings of the violin softly strumming around his heart.

The 'unavailable women' eagle eye 'single and available' colleagues of both sexes as who would be a suitable match for both. The 'unavailable women' conspire: PhD from north of the equator, Early Childhood Education; PhD from south of the equator, Adult Education. He drops in like a fallen leaf, she dances in as if to a Mardi Gras party. He is steadfast Jiān Dìng; she is happy Kuà Lè. He is proper, white shirted and blue trousered, dress shoes. She allows her metre-long three-tiered multi-coloured tresses to brush the air. Her smile is impish, she is ready to tease and has an interesting vocabulary of many foreign words that no one understands – well, maybe not everyone. A

Kam and a Goh, a perfect yin and yang, perfectly matched to make music as they sway hither and thither. Staff, however, are not unaware that Melissa and Charles arrive at work and leave together.

'Kam, have you invited Melissa on a date? Why not invite her home?' Mrs Ng suggests a few months later, sensing his agony on how to befriend Melissa, his abashed stammers even in his 'good morning', and his forlorn eyes following her and Charles in close proximity enjoying whispers, and laughing with abandon, oblivious to others.

'Date Melissa? We see each other five days a week.' He is surprised that he has to go on dates. Isn't seeing each other five days a week sufficient?

'I mean private time, just you and Melissa.' He could not disguise the pounding of his heart, sending gushes of blood to his face. 'If you're not comfortable with dates, why not write some beautiful notes. Put one in her tray. If she responds then it's clear she's interested.' Mrs Ng has plenty to offer.

Mrs Ng gives him several quotes. Kam studies them diligently, copies one and saves the rest for other days. He writes on a Mouth and Foot Association fundraising card in his neat writing in gold ink, and leaves it in Melissa's mail tray early the next morning.

> You are attractive, intelligent, creative and single.
> Kam

After lunch he stations himself at the office mailroom to check his tray, any reply? Late afternoon in she breezes, her hair caressing him. 'Hi, Kam darling, checking mail? Oops, mail for me. Tata. See you tomorrow,' and surges out as quickly.

That night Kam sees Melissa curled on the sofa, no, in her bed, in her striped-pink pyjamas, matching his blue one, reading his card, kissing the words, pressing it to her pounding heart, smiling and drifting into sweet dreams. Kam allows himself to fly into romantic exhaustion, believing he will get up with Melissa beside him.

Early next morning he rushes to the mailroom. His tray is empty. He feels a decade has passed when finally there is a reply for him later that afternoon. On the envelope, above where he has written 'Melissa', is written 'From', and a line is written below his note.

You are attractive, intelligent, creative and single.
Kam

I'm over qualified xxxxxx.

Kam, deliriously happy, belts out, 'Kisses for me, six kisses for me'. Mrs Ng, now his confidante, almost rattles off many six-letter words. Well, maybe 'x' here does mean kisses. She smiles. In the privacy of his room Kam closes his eyes, puckers his lips to suckle in the half dozen kisses. He researches kisses on Google and YouTube. He wants perfection when it comes breath-to-breath, nose-to-nose, lips-to-lips, tongue-to-tongue. Each day adds another six kisses. Before bed he slams his lips on his half-length mirror to practice the perfect kiss.

The exchange of notes continues. With each note, Kam is assured Melissa is his soulmate.

Follow your heart.
Kam

Brain is xxxxxxxx!

Since I met you, you've never left.
Kam

I need the $$$ xxxxxx

We don't meet people by accident, they are
meant to cross our paths for a reason.
Kam

What's your reason? What's your reason for all
this xxxxxx exchange? Can't just TALK????'
xxxxxx

Kam, much smitten with the boisterous Melissa, is happy to obey. He keeps all eleven notes in a pink gift box trimmed with purple lace. He sprays a mist of his cologne on each. Then he decides to talk to her.

The next morning, catching sight of Melissa and Charles, he calls out, 'Good morning, Melissa.' His heart pounds like a *roti prata*[64] chef punching his dough as he approaches her; it seems his little heart is about to break through the dough and flee. Melissa smiles ever so sweetly, 'Kam, darling, good morning.' He feels trapped, no turning back. She is tickled to see him now a beetroot. Finally he spurts, 'Melissa, what breakfast do you like?'

She is amused, such a mundane conversation starter. 'Oh, Charles enjoys local breakfasts.' The next morning he brings her a packet of *mee goreng*[65] in a plastic container. 'Shall we breakfast together? In the pantry. I hope you like this fried noodles. We have coffee 3-in-1. It's free.'

'Oh, Kam darling, how sweet.' She takes the noodles and turns to leave. 'Tata, going to class now.'

Kam has hopes of enjoying breakfast together but it does not happen. By the end of the week, *mee goreng, chee cheong fun*[66], *chwee kueh*[67], *nasi lemak*[68], and yam cake have been handed over.

'Kam darling, you spoil me, there's enough for two. We enjoy them.' But there is not a hint of who the 'we' are, no suggestion of 'Kam darling, let's breakfast together'. Yet the breakfast deliveries continue, this being Kam's 'talk' as he believes actions speak louder than words.

One morning she whispers, 'Kam darling, you don't want me to be round and an impossible hug, do you? No more

---

64 Indian flat bread, a breakfast favourite.
65 Fried noodles.
66 Steamed rice noodle rolls.
67 Steamed rice cakes with preserved radish.
68 Coconut rice, served with sambal, fried anchovies, toasted peanuts and cucumber.

breakfasts, ok?' The sweet melody of 'Kam darling' satiates him, 'an impossible hug' creates many amorous, sleepless nights. He drinks in her words like strong wine and enjoys feeling tipsy. He feels so much loved. And he loves from a distance. He seeks out Mrs Ng for love poems; Professor William Mason of the Music Department for romantic music. Bloom is un-Bloom-ed

At the University Day staff lunch, the dean decides it is befitting for staff to share 'something they had experienced during their university days, if they wish'. Melissa is delighted to share her first experience at a Maori party. 'Charles Apera and I were classmates. I spent warm summer evenings by the lake with Charles and his family. Mikaere, his father, prepared a traditional Maori delicacy of freshly roasted huhu grub. The grubs are the larvae of huhu beetles and live in dead wood in native forests. They are harvested and cooked for their protein and nutty flavour. Other traditional foods include whitebait, the seaweed *karengo*, *pikopiko* fern shoots, *karaka berries* and *toroi* which is a dish of fresh mussels and mud snails and downed with *pūhā*, a sow thistle juice. Oh, how romantic and serene to gather in the open, round the *hangi*, watching the little orange tongues of fire licking the open oven. The elders tell stories of how the gods create the earth, the trees, the lakes. We share the food, then we sing and dance. Charles gave me a Maori name, Whetu, meaning "star", because Charles says I am a star in his life. We slept in the fields, the stars and moon twinkling and smiling, giving us their blessings. I just love the Maoris. Mikaere blesses us, "'*ka hoki mai I'*, *aku tamariki*'". We promise Mikaere, we will, Charles and I will.'

Kam immediately shares his first Christmas party at university.

'Professor Martin reminded all his tutorial students to "bring a plate and a bottle". I thought, of course Prof won't have so many pieces of cutlery, so I brought a disposable plate, fork and spoon and my Tupperware tumbler filled with Ribena. I noticed everyone else brought food and beer and wine. That was a culture shock. Guests had to bring their own food and drinks? I taught Prof and my classmates Asian dinner invitation culture. Nonetheless I had plenty to eat and drink and we danced the twist. Several were drunk! I had a wonderful Christmas.' And he croons, 'It was so romantic', as he gazes at Melissa who is intensely engaged in communication with Dr Charles Apera Kingston, the only person who understands the implications of '*ka hoki mai I*' *aku tamariki*'.

Kam is determined to ask Melissa her choice of a partner. In his bedroom he studies himself in the mirror, from the waist up, practices his kisses, vocalizes several versions of his discourse, revises his body language, smoothens the white shirt and blue trousers. He has armed himself with a proposal she could not possibly refuse. He throws himself on his single bed and 'pillow talks' with Melissa but his bed is small for his vast expectations. He dreams of Melissa hunching over the hangi with that … that person … eating mud snails and ferns … sharing folklore, cuddling so unashamedly… too much to continue to dream on. It pains him that love brings such agony.

Yet, face to face with her along the corridor, breathing in 'Kam darling, good morning' he blushes furiously. He wants to wrap her in his arms and never let go. But first things first, he wants a serious chat with her on their relationship, yet his nerves are so fraught he shakes at the thought.

During the term break, Charles and Melissa are not seen in the office for ten days. Kam is disappointed, bewildered, distressed. He turns himself into a somnambulist with 'eyes wide shut' thinking on how to bag this woman. He goes about mechanically, his pain shovelling alongside him. Mrs Ng fears for his wellbeing, unsuccessfully tries to convince him Melissa is not worthy of his affection, a more romantic connotation in the realm of Jane Austen than love. Several colleagues believe he must have been an emotionally deprived child, not being called 'darling', thus his giddy obsession being addressed 'Kam darling'.

It is the end of the academic year again. The dean invites staff to a Staff Tea and Bonding. Wow! Kam is elated, perhaps that would be the right time to superglue himself to Melissa. The dean has a few announcements. Dr Charles Apera Kingston has accepted Chair of Dean, Cross Cultural Communication, Auckland University, and one colleague has resigned. Melissa waves her hand indicating her desire to speak, and sixty-five pairs of eyes pin on her, on what she will announce and to feast on the choice of words she would lavish upon Charles.

'My dear, dear Apera,' she begins. Kam's eyes open wide, his ears prick up. Has he heard right? 'Dear Apera, not Apera darling'? 'It's so wonderful you chose to join me here for a year. In university we were soulmates. With your family I was a sister, then a daughter. Your wonderful family taught me the simple happiness of family togetherness around the *hangi*, the flames never tired of dancing around it, warming our hearts. You taught me to dance in the rain, to love freely, to cry like a baby when my heart was broken. Last semester break we had the *haka* dance celebrations, uniting us, and with family and friends. Thank you Apera, for loving me so, so much. We love working here, but when it is time to go, we go. Charles and I, with your permission Dean, wish to sing a Maori love song, love for each other, love for family, love for community, love for country. *Pōkarekare ana* is a familiar song and please sing along. The lyrics are here.'

Charles turns on the DVD. Everyone knows the melody and sings along, several times over. Charles in his baritone voice is in perfect pitch. Even Kam sings along, his heart lifted, repeating one line '*Oh girl return to me, I could die of love for you*', not unnoticed by everyone.

Kam sheepishly observes Charles and Melissa hug and let go of each other. He feels liberated, ecstatic that there is nothing between them after all, it is a brother-sister relationship. The great sorrow he has inflicted on himself evaporates.

When tea is over, he voices, 'Melissa dar ... dar ... darling, dinner tonight, your place or mine?'

'Kam darling, let's go to Kopitiam across the road. Fish head *asam pedas*[69]. Charles enjoys fish head dishes, so much like home. We may not have such a dish again for a very long time. Our treat.' Kam holds out his hand, Melissa clings on to Charles's arm. He does not notice the ring on her finger.

---

69 A piquant spicy fish head dish.

Angel Cake

A young girl is caught in a complex family life. Parents aspire for their children to do better than themselves, to improve their lives. This is education. This girl has promised her parents she will continue school, despite having to help with chores. Her yearning for a cake was finally revealed and rewarded. The narrator is my friend.

Every morning I watch her step off Mosheng Bus number 329, walk along the row of eighteen shophouses, turn the corner to Convent Primary School. She starts with a lively step, swinging her satchel. Her steps slow at the eleventh shop, 73 Jonker Street. She pulls her leg one after the other, hand and face press on the glass panel, as she watches Hanny of Hanny Cake Shop arranging her freshly baked cakes on the stainless-steel shelves.

The glass panel reflects wide hungry eyes, fingers gingerly picking an imaginary slice of cake, tongue sweeping lips. She picks a different cake each day: a square chocolate, a green triangular *pandan*[70], a vanilla round, an orange rectangle from the four large shelves that stretch across the shop. Three large ten-tier stainless steel trays of cakes await their turn to pleasure the

---

70 Screwpine leaf.

palate. It is cakes, cakes everywhere. She enviously spies parents buying breakfast cakes for their children, at times teary. She waits for a customer to push the door open, then inhales the intense giddy orange, vanilla, chocolate, banana and pandan aromas, and she feels satiated. She caresses the cream cakes gently, afraid of disfiguring the curls and twirls of the different coloured cream, but never picks any of those. When Hanny catches her eye, she does her twister disappearance. At other times, she pulls her legs to school. She is there again after school. This time she points at the cakes, counting those left on the shelves, mimicking an accountant tallying the numbers. It appears that all she can afford is to look at the cakes. She is a such fixture over the two years Hanny has operated her shop that Hanny no longer notices the pre-teen schoolgirl at her window.

One day I decide to offer her a chocolate slice for breakfast. 'Good morning, have a cake.' She does her hurricane run through the crowd. I understand. Young girls are taught never to talk to or to accept any food from strangers, 'bad things will happen to you' if they do. But she intrigues me. Like clockwork precision, every school day she is there. I do it again the following week, the following and the following, enticing her with different flavours. No thank you, a voiceless decline then the twister run.

I have been friends with Hanny, lovely woman, almost all my adult life. She is my cousin's widow. We are partners in the cake business, but a stroke has stopped me from physical work. I do the accounts at the end of the day. I conspire with Hanny. When a customer pulls the door, and the girl's eyes close to pump her lungs with the aroma of freshly baked cakes, Hanny will offer her a slice.

'Hello, a nice slice of vanilla cake for a pretty, pretty girl.' She is so surprised she does her twister run but turns round once to eye Hanny. Perhaps Hanny is a motherly figure, and she feels less threatened. Perhaps she has never had such an offer. Hanny offers a slice of a different flavour each time; no words are needed. Finally, one day she whispers, 'No, thank you.' Her eyes say, 'Thank you, yes, I like that.'

'What's your name? How old are you?'

She turns and walks away, swinging her satchel, no twister run. A good sign. Now Hanny is curious too. Who is she? She has not given a thought to the girl who has peered through the glass panel to spy on her and the cakes. She has her own thoughts.

It is a ritual over the school term. She has noticed me sitting on the bench at the park across the road under the splendid Rose of India, boasting its canopy of lilac flowers during the hot season. It is a small park. Once she smiled, or I want to believe she smiled at me.

On the last week of the school term, she shyly stands at Hanny's window, wanting to catch Hanny's eye, hoping, I believe, Hanny's offer of a slice of cake still stands. She turns to look at me, perhaps appealing to me to get her a slice. Hanny smiles and beckons her inside. She accepts a cake. 'Can I take it home, please, aunty[71], please?' eyes pleading, afraid of rejection and the cake lost.

Hanny offers, 'Which flavour do you like most?'

'I don't know.'

---

71 In Asia, elders are addressed as 'aunty' and 'uncle' out of respect.

Hanny packs a vanilla slice, and carefully places it in a plastic carrier bag.

'Thank you, aunty, thank you.' The same exchange over the next days.

'Which flavour today?'

'I don't know. I have no money.' We ignore that confession.

'Banana slice?' Her eyes glisten, wetting the corners. She nods, to take home. It is the last day of the school year. Hanny gives her three slices, a speckled banana, a green *pandan*, and a rainbow vanilla.

I know I will miss her during the six-week end-of-school-year holiday. Hanny will too. We have grown accustomed to her face, seldom smiling, eyes, mouth and fingers caressing the cakes from a distance, ever so gently, fearful they might disintegrate and disappear. We name her Little Angel. She is pretty in a sad sort of way, a child carrying a weight, a cross.

I check the route of Mosheng Bus number 329. The bus starts at Jurong Bus Station and ends at Par Road Bus Station, a long route, 29 stops. Where are the stops? I do the route, note the stops. Jonker Street is the eighteenth. Of interest are 'LOVE Home', Stop 9, and 'Suchi Children's Home', Stop 11. No, I can't visit either, not being able to name the person I wish to visit.

Little Angel has grown taller when she turns up for the new school year. She looks more matured. She walks past Hanny Cake Shop. One afternoon after school, I wait for her at cake shop. 'Hello.'

'Hello,' and she walks away.

'Hanny misses you,' I call after her.

'I have to go.'

'Would you like a slice of cake to take home?'

'I can't. I just can't.' She does her twister run. The next day Hanny packs a chocolate, an orange and a walnut slice for her. She takes them without a word.

One afternoon, I am at the bus stop outside Suchi Children's Home, Stop 11. Sneaky, I confess. No, Little Angel does not alight there. The next day I am at LOVE Home, Stop 9. Little Angel alights with Hanny's cakes. She notices me, nonchalantly walks in. Who is there? Mother? Father? Sibling? I take the bus home.

Hanny and I have immersed ourselves with Little Angel. How can we impress upon her we want to be part of her life at LOVE Home, Stop 9?

Love is gentle, love is kind, love judges not, the bible teaches us. Over the month-long June holidays, Hanny invites Little Angel to help out at the cake shop. 'What do you want to know about LOVE Home, Stop 9?' she asks, quietly defiant. She is not a naïve child; she is a child woman.

That is when the dam shatters and floods her face. Her tears are from the storms inside her. Hanny's long arms are made to hug, to embrace, to love, besides kneading dough, beating eggs and arranging cakes on shelves.

'What's your name? How old are you?'

'My name is Lin San. 12 years. I'm in Primary 6. Next year I'll be in secondary school.'

'Would you like to talk about LOVE Home?' I ask.

'You were there, you spied on me. You were also at Suchi Children's Home. If you were James Bond you would have been dead.' And as an afterthought, adds, 'On your first mission!' The arrow hits the bull's eye of my core. I feel shame. How do I begin to tell her I am sorry? That I have violated her space? That Hanny and I only want to help? Who are we to want to help? Will she believe us?

Lin San's mother is in LOVE Home. She has been sick for a long time. A kind of flu, she does not know what. She can't stand, has poor appetite. Lin San and her father can't take care of her at home. Her nine-year-old sister lives with Nai-Nai, her paternal grandmother. Her father works two jobs, washing cars at the petrol station in the mornings, earning $3 for every car. Most days he washes three cars; automatic car washers have won over the business. From midnight to six he is a security guard at a condominium. He needs the money to pay for Mother's stay, and the school fees. They have no time to take care of Mother and sister at home.

'Where do you live?'

'With Mother. I sleep on the floor. The Home allows me, and I clean the Home every weekend. Mother eats very little, so I eat her share. I promise Mother I will never stop school. Father and sister sleep at Nai-Nai's house.'

'The cakes, what about the cakes?' Hanny asks gently.

'Mother worked at a bakery until she fell ill. She always brought the leftovers for us. She loves cakes.' Now we understand Little Angel's request to take home the cakes. Mother has told her she should not accept cakes or anything without paying for them. Everyone has bills to pay.

What is Mother's favourite cake? 'Angel Cake with a little

sprinkle of sugar dust. She's the specialist of angel cake. That's all Mother wishes for. A slice of angel cake, only one slice on Monday night when I can spend time with her. Weekends I'm very busy cleaning. Other days I study schoolwork. Aunty, you don't bake angel cake. Even if you do I don't have money to buy one. I can only look at the cakes and in them I see Mother.'

Hanny does not serve angel cake. A little slip with the eggs, the cake flops. That weekend Hanny and I work to bake the perfect angel cake. Many eggs have been laid in vain, as cakes flop. Finally, Hanny discovers it is the temperature of her oven. The angel cake is perfect, with a sprinkling of sugar dust.

On Monday, Hanny packs six whole pink angel cakes with a lacy ribbon tied round each. I take the bus with Lin San to LOVE Home. Hanny says there must have been a great celebration among the elderly at LOVE Home. We are sure there was. That night Hanny and I talk late into the evening. A 12-year-old girl has taught us, two matured seniors, what love and responsibility for family is.

In Towkay Lee's Mansion

'In Towkay Lee's Mansion' describes the daily activities of a Peranakan household as seen through the eyes of a ten-year-old Indonesian girl, whose Mak worked for the Lee family. She wondered why Mak, an educated professional, chose to work as a 'domestic help' when they had been comfortable at home. Not everything is as it seems.

Mak got a job in Towkay[72] Lee's mansion. She refused to talk about Bapa, my father, in the Lee household as it made her sad. End of Bapa, end of story. It was only Mak and I here in Singapore. Mistress Lee agreed to accept me though she complained loudly and when she was mad with whomever and whatever, she screamed, 'Employ one mother, two mouths come eat!' Towkay Lee was kinder. He greeted Mak and me cheerfully, 'Good morning, *selamat pagi*.'

One morning he asked, 'What's your name, little girl?'

'Rositawati.'

'Your name so *cantik*, so pretty, just like you. I call you Rosi, easier to say. Just like a rose, so pretty, so *wangi*, so nice smell like perfume.' I was happy now that I had a name in the house, not

---

72 Patriarch; boss.

'Girl'. I was a person with a name. I told Mak but she was not impressed.

Mak spoke little, silently doing what was asked of her. I believed she was sad to leave Bapa and her parents back in Surabaya. Bapa worked in a lawyer's firm. Mak was a teacher at the polytechnic. I was in school and Mak had applied for a one-year leave of absence from school for me. She had stated that I was to enrol in English lessons at the British Council in Singapore. I was very excited to go to Singapore. I wanted to ride the cable car, go to Gardens by the Bay, Sentosa Universal Studios, and learn more English.

Soon Towkay Lee patted me on the head, then on the cheek, then on the back. I was afraid to tell Mak that Towkay gave me $5 every time he patted me and said I was so *cantik*, so pretty. I kept the money between the pages of my book, in my school bag. It came in useful as the canteen food at British Council was expensive. I dismissed Mistress Lee's words as the idle chatter of a matriarch with a lot of unhappiness inside her. But I was careful not to upset anyone. Mak did the laundry and cleaned the house for them and taught Indonesian cuisine to Towkay's sister. Mistress Lee ruled over a household of eight: Towkay Lee and her; Young Master Lee, their eldest son; his wife Young Mistress Lee; Young Master Lee and Young Mistress Lee's eight-year-old twin daughters, Agnes and Amy, and a baby, Adrian. There was also Towkay Lee's youngest sister, who was the cook and single. She hardly spoke, moving silently cat like, so that when she cleared her throat, I jumped. I wished she would meow when she moved. She slept in a room adjacent to the main lounge, while Towkay and family had their suites upstairs. I do not remember her ever leaving the house. She was Rapunzel trapped in the kitchen. No prince had come her way, because she wore her hair very short.

Why, really why, did Mak choose to work here? I did not understand why Mak had to come to Singapore to work as a housemaid and cook. She explained that Towkay Lee's sister wanted to learn Indonesian cuisine. Mak taught her all about Indonesian cuisine, while the towkay's sister taught Mak her Peranakan cuisine, a sort of kitchen cultural exchange. Towkay Lee had wanted an educated and reliable teacher for his sister. Mak explained everyone had to eat, and to eat we had to work and when we worked we had money to buy food to eat so we would be alive. She confused me. We did eat in Surabaya. We ate *bakso*, beef-balls in spicy soup, *penyet*, crispy fried chicken, and Bapa took us to Japanese and Chinese restaurants sometimes. We had pizza and McDonalds and KFC too.

Mak's and my territorial space was the kitchen and the pantry where we slept. I was allowed to sit at the kitchen table after the day's work to do my homework. Mistress Lee's kitchen was large and handsome. It was adjacent to the dining room with its twelve-seater rosewood dining table. The first weekend I discovered the table could be pulled along its breadth to turn it into an eighteen-seater table. The tablecloth and table runners were batik pieces. On one side of the kitchen a wide door opened into the garden, where the gardener had planted herbs: pandan leaves, kaffir lime, curry leaves, chillies, *lengkuas, serai,* and in small planter boxes were *daun kesum* and *daun kemangi* for culinary needs. Beyond that were the rambutan tree, papaya, and banana plants.

On the opposite wall of the kitchen were stainless steel cabinets with several shelves. A Miele fridge with tens of magnets from countries visited, and a Miele dishwasher had their place beside the cabinets. The smaller Miele kitchen gadgets lived inside the cabinets. The stainless steel worktable was an island in the middle of the kitchen. I was surprised that the table, like the dining table, could unfold to extend it. Under the worktable were open shelves for different small-sized bottles of salt, sugar and pepper; different sizes of knives, long, short, big and small; chopping boards and washing-up liquid. At one end was a little DVD player for entertainment. Towkay's sister enjoyed keroncong[73] and Mak had brought six sets of DVDs for her. Her favourite was 'Bengawan Solo', played repeatedly until I felt suffocated and drowned in the River Solo. The Miele hobs and hotplates had their own place on the third wall beside the triple washbasins. To soften the harshness of the stainless steel, the walls were painted a soft bronze. The pale yellow ceiling lights created a harmonized tone for the kitchen, which gave it a pleasant warmth. The loud noise of the extractor fan, together with the pounding, cooking and keroncong formed an immense orchestra which transformed the kitchen into a lively Woodstock, a great contrast to the quiet living room. It was Mak's and Towkay's sister's turf, where they prepared every meal.

Our small kitchen in Surabaya was where Mak taught me the intricacies of the kitchen. We had a small TV on the wall. Mak's favourite chef was Gordon Ramsay. Our kitchen was a laboratory

---

73 A ukelele-like Indonesian musical instrument, and a musical style that often features the keroncong instrument.

where Mak taught me the spices for *pepes*[74], *sate kambing*[75], *sayur urap*[76]. Scrambled eggs were my favourite breakfast. Mak was pleased it was Gordon Ramsay worthy. It would be nice if Gordon Ramsay said it.

Lying on the thin foam mattress in the pantry, my back rested against the sacks of Thai Fragrant Rice Grade A, Jasmine Rice A, US Long Grain Rice, Basmati Rice A from India and Pakistan, brown rice, organic rice. I didn't know there were so many varieties of rice. On the shelves above were rows of extra virgin, virgin, cold press oils – olive, coconut, flaxseed, almond among others. The stainless steel pots and skillets cooled Mak's back. Other electronic gadgets fought for space above. I soon realised gadgets were not the only things edging one another out. On the upper shelves were tins of infant formula, cereals and milk. The cans of Australian abalone with price tags of $105 a can and packs of Premium Birds Nest at $2,800 for a 200-gram pack seemed to look down with disdain upon the cans of Yeo's Sardine in Tomato Sauce at $3.90, and pickled cucumbers in small bottles at $1.40 on the lower shelves. There were enough beverages to float Datuk's, my grandfather's, *sampan,* the small fishing boat he had built himself. If it had been slightly wider, the pantry would have resembled a mini market in my Datuk's kampong. Mak didn't mind the tight squeeze though and reminded me neither should I. That was my first experience sleeping uncomfortably on the floor but I felt wonderful in Mak's embrace. Now I understood why Mak and Bapa always slept together.

---

74 Fish or meat wrapped in banana leaf.
75 Goat satay.
76 An Indonesian salad of steamed vegetables with grated coconut.

We had plenty of food, leftovers from the family meals. Most of the food Towkay's sister cooked we did not like. Some, Mak said we could not eat. We had Indonesian dishes most days as Mak showed and taught Towkay's sister the intricacies of our cuisine. Mak said she was a good student. Mak never knew her name, they addressed each other *kakak*. I thought it strange as *kakak* meant elder sister. How could two women address each other elder sister? Mak brushed me off, 'Never mind.'

At night, Mak was busy writing in her notebooks. She had already filled one and was starting on a second. 'What are you writing, Mak?'

'Some recipes, new kinds of food. Nenek and Datuk I'm sure will like these new dishes.'

I wasn't sure my grandparents would like them. *Buah keluak* comes from Indonesia. Mak mashed some black meat of the keluak nuts into the spicy beef or chicken broth. *Rawon* is a family favourite for its spicy nutty flavour and dark broth. Mistress Lee cooked the black meat of the keluak nuts in spicy-sour gravy with chicken. Then there was *chap chye*, a stew of cabbage, carrots, and black fungus Mistress Lee called 'rats' ears' – they did look like rats ears, really; *itek tim*, a tart duck soup cooked with pickled salted mustard leaves; *meesua*, strange fine hair noodles cooked with pig liver and kidney, yucks! Mak and I did not eat the *meesua*. As I didn't like these foods, I was very sure my grandparents would not like them.

'That's our little secret and surprise for Datuk, Nenek and Bapa. Don't tell anyone,' Mak whispered. 'Mistress might not like us copying her recipes.'

One day I looked into Mak's notebooks. She had lots more notes than recipes. She drew pictures of Mistress Lee's sarongs and beautiful hip length *kebaya* blouses enriched with colourful embroidery of birds, fish, flowers and fruits. Mistress Lee had dozens of these *kebaya* and matching sarong skirts. She had several silver belts. She showed them to Mak. 'Let me teach you about our clothes culture. I have seven chain linked silver belts, all pure silver and the clasp is fourteen-carat gold. This three-inch-thick one is for important functions like New Year, weddings and birthdays. This one is lighter and thinner for daily home wear, this for going out, the others whichever I choose to wear. See the patterns of each link are different in each belt. This one is a fish looking up, this one a fish looking straight, these have three flowers and these two different birds.' She then went on to show us her collection of *kasut manek,* beaded slippers with their loud giddy colours. She explained the significance of the different patterns and colours. She muttered that young people no longer appreciated their culture. They preferred jeans, pants, cropped pants, T-shirts, tanktops, half-naked dresses and flip flops as well as five-inch stilettoes. 'Teach them a lesson. I'll sell all my antiques and jewellery. Nothing for them!'

That night I excitedly told Mak, 'Mistress Lee was so kind to tell us about her *kebayas,* belts, and slippers.'

Mak educated me on the sly ways of the matriarch. 'It was not to educate us, it was warning us she would know if we stole any of her valuables!'

Nonetheless, Mak had her writer's 'aha' moment. She wrote all that Mistress Lee told her about the significance of each pattern on the *kebaya*, on the belts, what colours were appropriate for which occasion. She checked with me the accuracy of what she had written. I conspired with Mak, 'I'll listen carefully to everything Mistress Lee said about her household. Perhaps we could publish a story when we get home and earn lots of money.' Mak was silent.

Mak drew pictures of the colourful Peranakan chinaware with its intricate patterns of dragons, phoenixes and chrysanthemums in different colours. She described the Thai rosewood prayer table, another piece of furniture with intricately carved sides and legs. On it were the daily offerings of joss sticks, and fresh flowers, and food offerings to the gods on 'special days'. That was Young Mistress Lee's responsibility. Mak asked Young Mistress Lee what the daily offerings meant and she was glad to chat with Mak when she had no lunch or tea appointments with friends. She preferred cropped and cut-off jeans and T-shirts – 'More comfy'. Mak wrote copious notes on each of her illustrations of chinaware that she had faithfully copied and coloured.

On Sundays, Towkay's siblings and their families came for lunch. It was the family tradition that the eldest son, as head of the extended family, ensured the ritual was kept. The kitchen was a beehive with mothers and daughters and daughters-in-law buzzing around washing, cutting, pounding, cooking and chatting. Queen Bee Mistress Lee decided on the menu, buzzed instructions on how to slice onions, chop the meat and how to cook each dish. She spewed stings to show her displeasure. At other times she dribbled honey to show favour to another. And Mak wrote many stories of the domestic affairs, the hushed tones of gossip, illicit affairs, the single Miss Lee who was the cook, why she was single, or was she, and why was she the cook; the fights and the celebrations, Towkay Lee's frequent business trips, what kind of business even his wife did not know about. I enriched Mak's writings with stories on Agnes and Amy, the twins.

I had responsibilities too. Three years older than the twins I was to be their shadow, to ensure they didn't hurt themselves, and to attend to their wishes. 'They are still babies,' Young Mistress Lee reminded me. At eight years old in Surabaya I was already boiling rice and cooking simple dinners for Mak and Bapa.

'I wish I could sleep in mummy's arms like you and your mother, Rosi,' Amy said sadly when she went to the pantry one afternoon. 'We have to sleep in our own room. We can't even sleep together. Sometimes I see ghosts, but Mother says I am just being silly. No ghosts in our mansion. Only Father can sleep with Mother and Grandma with Grandpa.'

Once, Amy suggested that they took turns sleeping with Mak while I slept in their bed. They would not tell anyone. Promise. 'Please *kakak*, just one night we sleep with you and you hold us in your arms, please.' Mak would have nothing of it. Agnes and Amy made me sleep in their bed once, to empathise with their loneliness. Mak did not say anything so that meant I could. I sank into the mattress, the blanket smelt like the roses in the garden, the room was large, cold, and as I merged into the darkness I felt abandoned. I saw ghosts as well, but was too afraid to scream and be discovered sleeping in Amy's room. I understood their need for their mother's warmth, why they felt sad. I was happy. Now in this grand mansion I have something they didn't have. I no longer envied their rows of Barbie dolls and clothes. Mak said nothing when I told her how sad Agnes and Amy were. Mak did not say much when I told her about the twins. She wrote them into her notebooks.

'Rosi, you are so lucky. You can stay in the kitchen and help cook.'

'Ya, we can't go into the kitchen, right, Amy? Grandma said knives have a life. And if we drop them they will come and sleep with us.'

'Rosi, let's play *masak-masak*.' But first they had to change into their play clothes. Their clothes were kept in separate closets – home clothes, play clothes, going out clothes, special occasion clothes. Same with their shoes, all of which matched their clothes. It was tiring when I had to wait for them to change into their 'right clothes for the right occasion' clothes. Why couldn't they be like Mak and me – T-shirt and pants all day until we took our bath at night, then a change into pyjamas for bed?

Amy did the marketing for our *masak-masak cooking games*. She picked choice rose stalks, and red, pink, white and yellow roses. Not even the gardener missed them. Agnes enjoyed being the cook, she *masak-ed* sand into fragrant rice, roses and ferns magically turned into stir-fried vegetables, twigs into strips of meat and water into soup. We had real dessert of fresh mangoes, rambutans, chikus and *jambu* during the fruit season. Large palm leaves were dinner and serving plates. I was served. I stole some dishwashing liquid from the kitchen and they washed the dishes with the garden hose, after which the dishes and leftover 'food' were thrown onto the compost. They were happy, we were happy.

One weekend, with much fanfare, the grand piano eased itself into the alcove of the sitting room. Young Master Lee proudly proclaimed, 'Ivory and ebony, like the piano keys,' as he placed an ivory miniature grand piano on the ebony piano. From then on it was casually referred to as Ebony. Young Mistress Lee was pleased. Music and piano skills would display the twins' grace in good society. My task was to wipe and polish Ebony with the piano cloth until it mirrored me. In Surabaya I wiped our piano with old T-shirts.

Teacher Pi An filled musical scores into the newly ordered ivory-coloured bookshelf. 'Mrs Lee, I guarantee you lovely Amy and beautiful Agnes will be the new-age Liberace, fingers fleeting across the blacks and whites (and in a lower tone) like mine. Within a year you will need another bookshelf for additional musical scores.' Only the grandparents and parents were pleased.

'People say I'm the best piano teacher in Bishan, Clementi and also Sembawang. What is a piano? Amy.'

'Teacher Pi An, you are a piano teacher and you don't now what a piano is? That one, beside you.'

'How many keys are there? Agnes.'

'I don't know. Front door keys, room keys, kitchen keys, cupboard keys ...' she giggled.

'Agnes, piano keys!'

Eighty-eight. Fifty-two white keys and thirty-sex black. I wiped them daily with the special piano cloth. They were clustered in 8s. From Middle C to the end of the left side the tone sounded lower and lower, while the right-hand keys rose to a higher pitch.

'People say I'm the best piano teacher in Bishan, Clementi

and also Sembawang. This is a clef, and this is a bass, symbols for right and left hand keys. Listen carefully I'll play this only once. What beat is this?'

'A drum?'

'My reputation is ruined! But I need to eat,' and his 'frustration' piece followed – 'Pretend You're Happy When You're Blue'. I didn't know that piece but I can play and sing 'Supercalifragilisticexpialidocious' superfast. In Teacher Pi An's class adagios and allegros intermarried; forte edged lento; staccato and legato were Best Friends Forever, chromatic scales confused octave. Young Mistress Lee had insisted the lovely twins learn music theory immediately. Teacher Pi An in his agony had to oblige, as he reminded us, he needed to eat, so he prepared basic worksheets. I needed another piggy bank for coins, a coin for each correct answer on theory worksheets.

'Mother, the theory room is cold and noisy and Teacher Pi An is the Wicked Witch of the East. He wouldn't let us go pee!' Ebony was abandoned, and Teacher Pi An was unceremoniously discharged but I still had to polish Ebony with the piano cloth daily. If only I was allowed to run my fingers on the keys, all eighty-eight of them.

Agnes and Amy were excited. They had watched 'Swan Lake on Ice' at the Esplanade Theatre. Agnes believed herself Princess Odette, and that was when the fight started – who would Prince Siegfried choose, Agnes or Amy. Young Mistress Lee was pleased. Nothing like ballet for posture and grace in young ladies of good families. The chauffer drove us to Belle's Ballet Studio. Young Mistress Lee had requested private lessons. 'Ballet lessons are always taught in a class,' Ms Belle Lee snapped.

'I want the white tutu.'

'Beginners, pink.' Ms Belle Lee was firm.

At the first ballet class, I packed their tutus, ballet shoes, hair nets to bun their hair, and water to keep them hydrated during the strenuous exercises. We had to change in the public washrooms, that first time.

Ms Belle Lee's studio proudly displayed dated life-size photos of her over the years teaching and winning awards. In her younger years she had danced Coppelia, Cinderella, Giselle, Odette and several others I did not recognize. 'Class, this is a slow exercise to test whether your posture is good, so make sure to keep your back nice and straight. Don't bend forward. And don't look down ever. Head and eye line nice and high.'

The girls stood in line holding on the bar on the mirrored wall and mirrored Ms Belle who held her posture and her breath for ten minutes. Ms Belle was kind, she knew it took practice and more practice and patience to do what she had done for thirty-two years.

'Watch me carefully. I'll do this slowly. Practice at home, one hour a day.' She did not explain how it was to be done. I told Young Mistress Lee to help practice balance and good posture, place an Oxford Dictionary on the heads as crowns and for a start, sit on stools for ten minutes, gradually increasing to twenty minutes. Then walk around slowly, not dropping Oxford.

'Mother, same, same, same. My toes ache, hands ache, tutu tickles. Our heads will shrink into our necks to our chest to our belly and pass out! Mother do you want headless girls? Ms Belle

Lee is the Wicked Witch of the West!'

'Darlings, you want to be swan princesses, don't you? Rosi, put Oxford on their heads, count to fifty. OK darlings. Love you both. Have to go now.'

'Mother, how can we practise without any guide?' Two Apple laptops, one for each girl, took their places in the large study room. The girls only had to login to You Tube and search for Ballet for Beginners for practice exercises. There were many.

'Mother, it's so boring. Why would I want to be a swan, ha?' Agnes in tears, mourned.

'Ya, Mother why would I want to be a swan?' Young Mistress Lee's unfulfilled dream as a child ballerina herself was shattered. She had to think of another sophisticated activity for her girls of a respectable family. Mistress Lee told her daughter-in-law not to pressure the girls, to let them take a break. Their genealogy already put them in good social standing. Mistress Lee's opinion always held.

The two Apples were stored in the storeroom together with the bird's nest.

Mak and I waited at the dinner table. At one dinner, Towkay Lee asked for extra virgin olive oil for his *sambal* pasta with lobsters and *petai*. I asked, 'What is extra virgin?' As I served him, he smiled, looked me straight in the eye and replied, 'You are extra virgin. And you are sooooo beautiful, Rosi.' He fed me a little of the pasta with a dash of extra virgin olive oil and patted me on the cheek. It tasted yucky and I told him so. I was never present at the dinner table again.

Two months later Mak told me that Towkay's sister had

learnt all she wanted about Indonesian cuisine. We could go home to Bapa, Datuk and Nenek. We had been away for ten months. Agnes and Amy begged to go with us. I was sad to leave them. We had become close friends, a sort of sisterly bonding. I was also happy to go home to Bapa, Datuk and Nenek. I was sad as I had to sleep in my own bed in my room, no Mak to embrace. I was happy to eat bakso again. Agnes and Amy gave me their laptops. Young Mistress Lee was nonchalant about them giving away both Apples, one for me, and one for Mak. The iconic bite had not a byte in it. It would help Mak writing her notes.

Three months after we arrived home Mak submitted her M.A. thesis *Peranakan Culture: A Case Study in a Peranakan Household* to the University of Indonesia.

First published in *The Best Asian Short Stories 2020* (Zafar Anjum, ed.) Singapore: Kitaab (2020)

Silent One

In the past, poor Chinese families sometimes gave away baby daughters to rich households as servant girls or bondmaids. They believed and hoped their daughters would have a better life. The babies were left nameless, with no birth certificates. The adoptive parents referred to them as 'chabor', 'girl', or 'chaborkan', a variation of the Hokkien word and used in Peranakan households to refer to bondmaids. A sympathetic household might adopt them legally.

I never knew my parents or where I came from, or how old I was. In the big house they called me Chabor. So I was Girl, nothing more. Everyone addressed the gentleman of the house Ye-Ye Chai, grandfather Chai, and Nai-Nai, grandmother, was the mistress of the house. They relished the honorifics, which bestowed stature as patriarch and matriarch, caring for their household staff and other employees. However I did not think they were old enough to be grandparents. They did not even have children!

Nai-Nai said she took me as a newborn because my parents did not want me and used that to humiliate and mentally torture me. She did not know who my parents were or where they were from. A woman had come to her house and asked if she would adopt me, and she did. Ah Hanjie, a 'white and black[77]' head servant and three other general servants were tasked to look after me, until I could make myself useful doing chores. Ah Hanjie cradled me when I was sick or frightened or bullied by the other servants. They called me bad names, cursed my mother, but Ah Hanjie was kind and gentle. She taught me to sing Cantonese songs. The household spoke a mixture of Cantonese and Hokkien, local Chinese dialects. Ye-Ye and Nai-Nai were fluent in English as well. In the big house I was the only child, so logically I should have been loved and spoilt, shouldn't I? I did love Ah Hanjie. She offered to be my mother. It was so nice to have a mother in the big house. I was the only one with a mother. I had never seen or heard anyone talked about Ye-Ye or Nai-Nai's parents.

During one of Ye-Ye's birthday celebrations I asked Mother, 'When is my birthday? I want a cake, a big one like Ye-Ye's.' She did not know.

'You came to this house on the 8th, so we take 8 July as your birth date.'

'Why 8? I was born before 8.'

'Eight is a good number. In Chinese, eight is the same sound as 'luck, good fortune'. Now your fortune is not good, you are a servant girl, but who knows the future?' So 8 July was my birthday, but still no cake.

One birthday I went to Nai-Nai, 'Nai-Nai, today is my birthday. I want a big cake, like Ye-Ye's cake.'

I got a big kick instead and was screamed at. 'You are a

---

77 These domestic servants, known as majie, wore a distinctive uniform of a samfoo with white blouses and black pants. They swore their loyalty to their employers and remained unmarried.

nobody, even your mother did not want you! She abandoned you. There is nowhere you can go. You are nameless, person-*less*, no birth certificate, no nothing. So I can do anything I want with you. You chabor, my servant, will live here forever!'

That night I told Mother when I grew up I would be a Nai-Nai and throw her out!

I babbled a lot, asking for things, teasing the cats and dogs and the servants. Sometimes a servant reported to Nai-Nai what I did or said or when I broke something and Nai-Nai spanked me, usually with a broom. It was so unfair! I hated her, and her diamonds and her painted nails, and makeup, all compressed into her pantsuit, like an anaconda that had swallowed a crocodile. I made faces at the servants, pinched them, and ran away. I was too fast for them to catch me. Mother impressed upon me to speak little. My silence kept me out of trouble. Silence, my friend. So I was silent most of my growing up years. I talked only to Mother. In whispers. But I listened, listened to what everyone said, and watched what they did, and I learnt. Thus my moniker 'Silent One'. Soon Ye-Ye too called me Silent One. But to Nai-Nai I was just *chabor*, servant girl, nothing more.

Nai-Nai said my hands were large enough to massage body parts – large but still delicate. Mother taught me to gently massage hands and legs, and to 'flap', that is to gently tap aching muscles. At four years old, I was flapping Nai-Nai's shoulders and arms. Ye-Ye however preferred me to massage his legs, thighs, hands, arms, and flap his back. Ye-Ye took off his shirt and wore only his pyjama pants when I massaged and flapped him. He explained that my hands were not strong enough for a good massage and flap if he kept his clothes on. Sometimes he turned round for me to flap his abdomen. When I was about ten years old, he pointed to 'that thing' below his abdomen and asked if I knew what it was. I didn't. He said that made him a man. 'Girls don't have them, but when they grow up, they want that thing. Men must give girls that thing when they want it. When you become a woman, I will show you my thing and you will want it too. I will give it to you.' After each massage he gave me a chocolate and we ate it together. The chocolate, our little secret. I was happy. He also gave me a proper name, Orchid Chai. That was our secret too, not to share with anyone.

When I was eight, Ye-Ye had a private tutor teach me Maths, English and Mandarin. Nai-Nai screamed, 'Chabor, servant girl, don't waste money!'

Ye-Ye explained that I would be able to help the business reading letters, writing simple reports, doing simple accounts and other administrative tasks, as all his gardeners were barely literate and not to be fully trusted. Nai-Nai was not happy. After every lesson she asked me, 'Chabor, what did you learn today? Waste my money!' When I could not respond fast enough, she slapped me, sometimes kicked me. She did not understand that sometimes I could not follow the lesson. That made me more determined to study well.

My English teacher was the best. He taught me a lot about how to speak, read and write. The storybooks were my best friends. One day I would be one of the Famous Five in Enid Blyton's books. I would go on adventures like Anne and have a dog like Timmy, my best friend. He would do what I asked of him, 'Timmy bite Nai-Nai.' I saw her screaming and running like a headless chicken in three-inch sandals. I gave Timmy a thumbs-up. And I read many more books. Ye-Ye gave my tutor money to buy all the books I wanted. My English teacher also bought me a book he said should be my 'lifetime friend', the Oxford Dictionary, a big fat book too heavy to carry, but weightless in my head.

As I grew older, everyone in the big house was suspicious that Ye-Ye needed daily massages and flaps in his locked study room where he had a large daybed. I told Mother that Ye-Ye wore only his pyjama pants, she was sad. I did not tell her about the chocolates, my new name or Ye-Ye's 'that thing'. He had said it was for me only.

Mother warned me, 'You are a poor, servant girl. Nai-Nai can punish you and even throw you out anytime. Be careful not to let Ye-Ye touch you.'

'Why, Mother?' She did not tell me why. The other servants looked me in the eye whenever Ye-Ye asked for massage and flaps and sniggered when I came out of the room. But no one said a word, not even Mother.

Ye-Ye Chai was the owner of Chai Orchids the largest orchid farm in Pahang, Malaysia. One day he took me with him to his farm, an hour's drive away from his house.

Nai-Nai was suspicious, 'What can chabor do at the farm?' Ye-Ye explained that my little hands would be gentle and delicate with his prized orchids, Cattelyas of all species and colours. That was also the first time I sat in a car. It was so wonderful, the wind in my face, the different scenery.

The orchids were so beautiful that I spontaneously plucked

a slightly opened white bloom with blushing pink lips to tuck into my hair. The gardeners gasped in speechlessness, one quickly pulled it away, squinted around to ensure no one else saw what I had done. But Ye-Ye saw. He tucked the bloom into my blouse button, patted me on the cheek and bellowed, 'This time OK, one more time not OK!' The menacing look made me pee in my pants.

Head Gardener Li pinched me hard on the arm and whispered, 'Silent One, one more time you pluck orchid I throw you inside manure. No one find you! You die, you die!' Gardener Li was to teach me about packing the orchids. My small delicate hands were perfect to pack the fragile blooms for export.

The farm had a small house. It had a room with two beds in the corner, a small table and four chairs, a toilet, a small fridge and kettle and a few pieces of cutlery, lots of chocolates and snacks. I could have them. In the afternoons Ye-Ye said I could rest there till we went home. Sometimes he rested there, he and I, on one bed each. I liked it there, the serenity, the chirping birds, the beautiful trumpet tree. No Nai-Nai to order me to do chores or to hit me. No servants to find fault with my chores. Only Mother protected me from their taunts of 'sayang sayang, nice nice, ya?' with Ye-Ye. I didn't know what they meant.

One day I cried, I thought I was going to die. I was bleeding in my pants. Life was hard, but still I did not want to die. Mother told me that I must be eleven years old or so, and I had become a woman. She taught me all I needed to know about being a woman and taking care of my personal hygiene. My breasts were showing too. Ye-Ye noticed. He took me to the farm more often and spent more time in the little house, resting with me.

On one visit, when I was sixteen there was a thunderstorm. He gave the gardeners the afternoon off. He would lock up. We could not go home yet. Gardener Li thanked Ye-Ye, smiled broadly, and looked at me straight in the eye. Alone, Ye-Ye reminded me about 'that thing' he had. I was curious and nodded. Amidst the furious pounding of the rain, spasmodic roaring thunder and flashes of lightning, Ye-Ye taught me what it meant to be a woman, for a man and woman to please and enjoy each other. The night was naughty and wet and loud. He did not warn me of the consequences.

We stayed at the farm more often. Mother asked me what happened. I snapped, 'Ye-Ye wants me to work on the farm. I can read and write English and Mandarin, and do math.' Period. She knew. I felt privileged. I felt loved. I felt superior. Superior over Nai-Nai, that barren woman, superior over Mother in her uniform of white blouse and black pants, and the servants in their *samfoo*, all barren women, all servants, all their lives. Ye-Ye wanted me, not them! Ye-Ye also bought me pretty dresses, 'office clothes' he explained.

Nai-Nai knew. Ye-Ye knew she knew. The servants and gardeners knew. Everyone knew. Then Nai-Nai threw me out. Such was the fate of a *chabor*. Who cared about a servant girl? The driver put me on the train to Penang, to the Snake Temple, as a servant to a friend of Nai-Nai's friend. She had hoped the numerous snakes would kill me and mine. The driver advised me, 'Study the snakes. Snakes in the temple may look lethargic, but they are not. They use their hypnotic eyes, their silence, their hearing, their speed to strike. Be friends with them.' He hugged me, too tight, his chest crushed my breasts, pinched me on the cheek, smiled through his tobacco-stained teeth and added, 'Take care of yourself and ... and others.'

Ye-Ye where are you? In the Snake Temple I watched the snakes, their patient, silent slithering in the dark, listening intently for movements, eyes focussed on the prey, and their lightning strikes. Success always. Good strategy. They had baby snakes, hatched out of eggs. Sadly, baby snakes were taken and kept aside, I wasn't sure why. However, eventually they were brought back to their mothers when they had grown a little. In the temple I was alone, I enjoyed being alone, just me and mine, for a while. Nobody could hurt me. This break away from everyone allowed me to figure everything out. I thought I wanted to disappear, but I really wanted to be found. I wanted revenge. I talked to my only true companion, Oxford and it demonstrated what revenge is:

/rɪ'vendʒ/ [uncountable] something that you do in order to make somebody suffer because they have made you suffer. revenge for something She is seeking revenge for the murder of her husband.

I needed to punish Nai-Nai for beating me, kicking me, cursing my mother whom I did not know. For sending me far away from my Ye-Ye and mine. Revenge was dancing in my mind. Each day the dance got better.

Two years later, Ye-Ye came for me. Now I lived in the little garden house beside the trumpet tree. The house was larger, more modern and a little kitchen had been added. Everything there was new. There was a small bookshelf filled with books. I loved it. I loved Ye-Ye and we loved ours. I did not step into the main house again till years later. Everything about me had changed. I had hoped to see Mother. For years I was abandoned, she, my mother could not find me. So, it was over, Mother and I. I was twenty-one, a full woman with a man and a child not like her, always a servant without a man.

Gardener Li, all smiles, welcomed me with a hug, too tight, his hands stained with manure. There were new gardeners. I was now a new gardener, an apprentice, not an orchid packer. Ye-Ye's menacing body language, fiery voice, and piercing eyes silenced everyone at work. At other times when we slept in the garden house, he was gentle. We talked of love, children, and many things.

Head Gardener Li was tasked to teach me everything about orchid cultivation. 'Silent One, Chai Orchid farm most big in Pahang, second big in whole Malaysia.' I knew that. He continued, 'Most big one Sarawak. Sometimes Ye-Ye go buy orchids. You got go? You learn good, you become *towkay* of farm, girl boss,' he laughingly insinuated. What did I learn? The names of the orchids, the potting media, the amount of water needed, when to water, the fertilizers used, recognising a mature stalk ready for picking, storing and packing.

We ate our lunches and early dinners under the shade of my favourite trumpet tree. It was spectacular during the dry spell when pink and white blossoms covered the entire tree. It then scattered its winged seeds. Similarly, I had blossomed, had trumpeted my fertile femininity, and had received the winged seeds, ready to germinate again.

Mealtime talk was mundane most times. At other times, the gossip was about Ye-Ye and his household. Head Gardener Li was the information disseminator, everyone else listened. 'Silent One, you can talk, talk something. You long time you live in big house you know many thing. I tell you little bit about Ye-Ye everyday, so you understand Ye-Ye and Nai-Nai.' I understood the family. When Ye-Ye was not at the farm, they talked about the Chai household, Nai-Nai, their wealth. I suspected they wanted to trap me. No, they couldn't. I was liberated in my silence. No questions to answer, no explanations expected, no lies required. My silence was my weapon.

'Silent One, you like stay here? Like work here?' I nodded, though I was on the verge of responding. I smiled. Smiles never hurt anyone.

'Silent One, you young girl. This man work. Girls not strong, cannot work so hard.' I couldn't take the labour? I laboured eight hours! Alone. In Penang. The fruit of my labour was worth the pain. Where is my fruit? My fruit was stolen from me when he was six months old, when I was told I had to strengthen myself with herbs at another temple and my fruit would be taken care of by a nursemaid. Everyone there was 'Silent One' like me. I only had story books delivered to me, regularly, anonymously. It was from Ye-Ye. And I had Oxford. I cringed and surprised myself when I shed tears that night, the first time I cried since I came home to the farm alone. My anguished screams were silent.

'Ye-Ye, he good man. He take good care of us. When we sick, he ask driver take us go see doctor, and he pay doctor, we no need work one week, still get money. We get big *angpau*[78], sometimes $500 when business good. Chinese New Year, always get big *angpau*. Also we go famous restaurant eat big dinner. Best *yu-sheng*[79] in whole world. Good fortune *yu-sheng* with good fish and abalone. He order many plates. Also got pork, chicken, and many food. Also can drink beer. We all like. We eat plenty.'

'Silent One, you afraid stay garden house, one person night time? So quiet no one disturb you.'

Another gardener cut in, 'If you afraid I sleep with you.' Everyone laughed, a sniggering, knowing kind of laugh, with slapping of backs and thighs and tables, and kicking of legs.

In the silence of the night I wanted to be disturbed. Ye-Ye was never quiet.

Gardener Li continued, 'About four years ago Nai-Nai go round world holiday long time. Got money, no children, can go holiday many months. And she come back with one baby boy. Some say she take baby from China. Some say Ye-Ye cannot have baby, so Nai-Nai go China and ... you know, got baby and Ye-Ye tell lawyer want to make baby his son. Some say baby Ye-Ye's real baby. His name Chai Hong Seng. Now baby over three years old already. Silent One, this true or not?'

I cherished the joy of Seng suckling on my breasts for six months in Penang. Then Nai-Nai stole him. I will have him back! He's mine!

'True or not ah, Nai-Nai no trust you stay in big house anymore? When you small girl, you stay there. Now you cannot

---

78 Red packet, a gift containing money.
79 A Chinese New Year dish of raw fish and shredded vegetables eaten in Singapore and Malaysia and which symbolizes good fortune.

even stand outside house. She say you dirty, you have nothing, you steal her money and many things. Then you run away because you steal her gold chain. She say she very kind not report you to police.'

I nodded and smiled. If only they knew! I and mine were the stolen ones. I was glad I was the Silent One. They cajoled me into telling my story. My silence was power.

'Silent One, you got see your baby? Oh, oh sorry, sorry, sorry. You got see Ye-Ye Chai son? He very cute one, eyes small, like yours, hair also very curly. Same your hair also very curly.'

'Ye-Ye got tell you about baby?' Did he need to?

How I longed to see my son. One afternoon Mother brought us our lunch. She beckoned me over to the car. There he was, in the baby chair, *my* son. Ya, eyes small like mine, hair curly, like mine. Son, you are well taken care of. I love you very much. I love you from a distance. We'll be together soon. Promise. Mother and I did not speak. She held my hand for a moment. I wished she had hugged me, or at least smiled. Perhaps she also despised me.

Gardener Li was concerned about my condition. 'Silent One, you vomiting many times every day. Morning you vomiting plenty times. Tell Ye-Ye take you go hospital see doctor. But you now also more fatter.' He patted me, condescendingly. He knew. All knew. The other gardeners in turn encouraged me to tell Ye-Ye I was not well. Their concerns for my welfare said what they could not say.

'Silent One, you sick, your face also like white. But you also more and more fat every month. Something growing inside your stomach. Go see doctor, tell Ye-Ye take you go see doctor.'

'Silent One, you cannot walk properly. Please, please tell Ye-Ye you very sick. Something in your stomach so big. You afraid tell him. He good man. He can see your stomach big, you sick. You cannot walk properly. Tomorrow I go tell him you sick.' Head Gardener Li comforted me. Comfort or snigger or contempt, I didn't care anymore. I have another son.

What would I tell them? How could I tell them? Ye-Ye know I was the fresh white bloom with pink lips and he had blown into it.

That night, I took one last look at my orchids, my trumpet tree, my little garden house. We walked out. I was bent over holding my belly tight, wet between the legs. Ye-Ye held me tight.

Six months later Li informed the gardeners the latest Chai household news. Silent One had returned to Ye-Ye's house. She was sick and Nai-Nai had sent her away to Penang to rest. 'Ye-Ye go lawyer office sign paper adopt another baby boy. His name Chai Hong Thian. The first boy name Chai Hong Seng. They are brothers. Real brothers.

'Ye-Ye also say Silent One stay in house can take care of Seng and Thian. She young and healthy and very motherly. She love them very much. She now second Nai-Nai. Old Nai-Nai *boh pian*, no choice, she no give Ye-Ye son or daughter. Now she afraid Silent One.'

All mothers love their children, don't they? I have metamorphosed beautifully from an unwanted, unnamed *chabor* servant girl to Silent One to Orchid Chai to Second Nai-Nai. Soon to complete the metamorphosis into a Monarch Butterfly.

That Saturday Night Dance

This story is based on a true incident – four lifelong friends and the tragedy that happened one Saturday night long ago.

Pansy reminds us to dress up and bring out the bling. She has invited us to an al fresco dinner by the sea at the newly renovated Happy Land Hotel where Ocean View Hotel once stood.

6.30 SHARP! HONEST! her message reads.

At 6.30 we are there, though we don't expect her to be. She is never on time.

'Does anyone really expect Pansy to be here to welcome her guests?' Wan mutters.

'No, she hasn't been on time for even one of our monthly lunches since she returned home,' I say. 'And still the same pride; only she can pick up the tab.'

'Mary, we have excellent lunches, free of charge! For three years almost!' Kim responds, smiling.

'6.30 sharp? Oops, really? 8.10 already? I don't have a watch,' Kim mimics Pansy. 'We bought her a SEIKO watch for her 21st birthday. And what did she say? "Thank you, girls. My philosophy is to never wear a watch. A watch doesn't compliment being dressed up, unless of course it's a Cartier."'

'Pansy, you don't wear a watch as an excuse to be late,' I had once said, 'and because you are super rich!' I had been envious of her wealth. I hated her disdain for 'those poor things' – that is, us. Wan and Kim had looked at me in surprise. I surprised myself. Pansy did not take offence, instead she turned the tables on us, gave us nicknames and still we did not protest. I had always been the quiet one, 'half sentence girl' or 'half-sentence Mary', then there was 'giggly Wan' and 'long-discourse Kim'.

'What about you, Pansy?' Wan had enquired.

'Oh, I'm just me, "bling, bling, the real thing, Pansy".' She didn't batter an eyelid. 'My philosophy is a late entrance creates a pause in the gathering; everyone looks at you. When you are dressed, bling bling and all, you are the focus of attention. It's a great feeling.'

Tonight, Pansy has reserved a table near the water's edge, and we are seated under an attap canopy in comfortable cushioned rattan chairs waiting for her to arrive. The waiter serves us a complimentary fruit punch. We look at one another and laugh.

Kim bursts into a melodious mantra, 'Same, same good old days. The same tradition, a free Coke or 7Up first drink, and prices doubled after ten! Our dates, in turns, ordered three rounds of Coke and 7Up for each of us before ten! Sometimes it was orange or lemon juice. Let's drink up then, we drink the real thing!'

'We lost Pansy for forty years. Since she came home, she's not been the showy Pansy we grew up with,' Kim hisses.

'She's more sober,' Wan replies. 'I wonder why she chose this place?'

'Gossip has it that she has never fully recovered after that ...'

'None of us have, I think. Have you, Mary?'

I whisper, 'Any of you been here since, since ...' Silly girl. Of course we haven't.

'What is still familiar to you?' asks Wan. 'Only the sea, the moon and the stars. This dining area was the dance floor. Not quite the same old tiled dance floor, ya? Remember every hour or so when the band took a fifteen-minute break, a hotel staff "talcum powdered" the floor. We never knew the reason for it. This polished deck floor is much better-quality wood. It's also larger and the music croons invisibly.' Wan is chirpy.

In silence we scan the open-air dance floor where the live band played nighty in the gazebo. We danced there every Saturday night when we were young, newly employed professionals. Pansy wanted us there. We called it The Summer Place, after Sandra Dee's hit movie of the same name. Everyone wanted to be Sandra Dee, not because of Sandra Dee but because she got the most handsome boy. We wanted that boy. Another time we wanted to be Maria and marry the Captain with seven children; the list of films continued.

'The lady in the floral dress, you think the gazebo ...' I ask no one in particular. 'Pansy's favourite table ... the angsana tree, front row. The tree's gone, the gazebo's gone, the band's gone. Nothing of what I remember is left.'

'Pansy always had her way. What she suggested, we did, rather, we obeyed.'

'Yes, Wan. Why did we?' I feel bitterness rising.

'Because we were poor. And because your father was the

accounts clerk in her father's company ... clerk, ok, not an accountant. And our mother was the chef in her mansion. That's why!' Wan snaps back.

Kim rationalizes, 'We were well looked after, right up to uni. Her dad even gave us an allowance. Look on the positive side.' Kim and Wan are inseparable twins. 'We are grateful for that. Her dad was a great, compassionate man. With Pansy, the spoilt brat, as the only daughter. And our parents told us to be nice to Pansy, always. We were the same age, in the same class.'

'Same brains, without tuition, without anything.' Again I feel resentment.

We remember the new clothes we wore were Pansy's old clothes. One Chinese New Year I had to wear the new dress she hated.

'I hated that yellow dress with red polka dots, I never wore it again,' I say.

The twins laugh. 'At least you got a new dress.'

Wan recalls, 'Pansy once said to Tony, "Tony, that hair clip, earrings and pendant I gave Wan. Looks good on Wan, right? Wan in want." And she giggled. Tony did look uncomfortable but said nothing. Tony, Tony, what really happened?'

'She made us feel inferior, it gave her power over us! Why do we still hang out with her?'

'Our parents were glad they did not have to buy clothes, shoes, and other girlie things for us.' Kim rationalises. 'And we have grown accustomed to her face. And her father's generosity towards our parents and us.'

'I guess we were friends from school to university, when we

were young professionals and now in our senior years,' Wan continues.

'But why do we still defer to her?' says Kim. 'I've asked myself several times. I have no answer.'

'I guess we share the guilt. Many times I see her as "poor thing". How ironic, when she had referred to us poor things.'

'And this was where we danced every Saturday evening. With our boyfriends. And only Tony paid all the bills, because Pansy insisted.'

'We had boyfriends. Where are they now? Not one of the four around.'

'Remember the bandmaster?' I say. 'He always started the evening with *"Welcome friends. This evening we play as always your favourite dance music. It will be an evening you will never forget."* Then straight away his signature song "Begin the Beguine".'

I hum then Wan and Kim hum along. We remember those opening lines to start the dance, how could we not? Pansy and Tony, the perfect pair, the same physique, the same social status, the same interests and the same boldness. They laughed without restraint, embraced without embarrassment, danced only with each other and raced their cars without a care. We were terrified to ride with them. But only Pansy and Tony had cars.

'Yes, Mary, it was always the same. "Begin the Beguine", a beautiful rhumba. We were on our feet. And with "Goodnight Irene" when the evening was over, till next Saturday evening.'

'"Goodnight Irene" our Cinderella hour. But tea dances began with "Tea for Two" cha-cha-cha, more lively music, more rock and roll, jive, limbo, twist,' Kim reminisces.

'That's because it was bright sunlight! No arms locking please.' We laugh at Wan, her hands embracing herself.

Those were the days. We often wondered why the bandmaster addressed us 'friends' instead of 'ladies and gentlemen'. We concluded that he was aware that many of us were not quite ladies and gentlemen, but giggly young people, perhaps a little foolish too.

'Kim, your favourite song was "My Little Corner of the World". You were secretly in love with the bandmaster! You wanted a little corner with him, didn't you? And your date was Teck!' Wan winks mischievously.

'Alfonso was his name. He was Portuguese and had a gold front tooth. I wonder where he is now?' Kim sighs. We wonder too. Probably deceased. 'Pansy had to have the seat facing the sea. Where is she anyway? Same, same Pansy.'

'Oops, sorry, no watch,' I snigger.

'Hi, hi!' Pansy waves from a distance. There she is, in a little red buttoned-down dress, shoulder-duster jade and diamond earrings, matching pendant and a sheer Hermes scarf, carelessly tied round her waist instead of her neck, as she always does. Our 'bling bling'? Large pieces of paste masquerading as ten-carat gems.

'Am I late?' That is an understatement. 'Em, I said 7.30, right? So ten minutes late is not late, right?'

'No, Pansy, see your message. 6.30 SHARP! HONEST! All in caps,' I snap. 'And we believed you.' At seventy plus years old I do not have to be deferential to her.

She pretends not to have heard. 'Oh, Mary, Wan, Kim it's so nice to get together here. It's been quite a while since we met here. Kiss, kiss, kiss ...' she blows to each of us. 'Wow, Mary, such large bling bling.'

'Can't afford small bling bling, so got large ones!' I feel incensed.

Pansy hums then softly sings, *'Those were the days my friends, We thought they'd never end. We'd sing and dance forever and a day, We'd live the life we choose, We'd fight and never lose, For we were young and sure to have our way.'* Her earrings sway with her.

'Now, we are no longer young.'

'Wan, stop that. It's all in the mind, your mind. We're here to have a good time. To reminisce about those days? No, thank you. Now, let's drink! No 7Up, no orange juice.' Pansy has pre-ordered pre-dinner drinks. Dom Pérignon, no less. 'I'm starved. Eat, drink and be merry, for tomorrow we die. Now who said that? Ahh, who cares?'

'I think it's from some bible passage. Not sure which.'

'Mary, you were always a holy holy girl. Always praying. You should have been a nun. But I guess you also wanted sex!' It is hurtful. And ironic too.

Kim comes out fierce, 'Pansy, stop it! We wanted sex, that's why we got ma ...'

Wan, giggling Wan, taps the table, stands, wolf-whistles and points her hands to her mouth gestured to the waiter for the menu.

Pansy is chirpy and humming bits of melody. Her emerald shadowed eyes rotate like an owl's, seeking a prized picking. It appears that by talking and humming continuously she might eventually let loose something within her, not yet sure when it will be appropriate.

'Pansy, remember your angsana tree? You always had to have the seat facing the sea.'

'Yes, I did, Kim. The moonlit sky, the silent, seductive call of the sea, the smell of the salt, the sands kissing my feet, so romantic. Secretly I wanted to throw off my clothes and swim forever, with Tony of course. Throw caution to the wind, like the girls and the limbo rock.'

'Throw caution to the wind but not your clothes, ya? And why didn't you? You were always on the wild side. Do you have your bra on today?' Wan giggles. Pansy had once dared us to not wear a bra to the dance.

Pansy releases two buttons of her dress. 'Red Triumph push-up! All real!' she boasts coquettishly. 'Tony, I told him, we'll send you home, then return and jump naked into the sea. He said we'd drown. How ironic!' Pansy reminisces sadly, then her scarlet lips curve into a smile. 'I'm here to celebrate with you, my long-time friends. I'll tell you after dinner.'

We eat our dinner of black ink pasta, beef stroganoff, roast duck a l'orange, poached lobster and waldorf salad, more sophisticated than the fried noodles or rice of fifty years ago. We raise our glasses of cabernet sauvignon and Dom Pérignon in silence, four kids then, now silver haired seniors.

'Lovely evening', I whisper lamely, 'the pasta was yummy.' That is not what I had planned to say. My words roam in my mind with no way out.

'I have to get this out. I really do. All these years, it trapped me like a little devil piggybacked me whispering, *Swim, swim, swim*,' Pansy suddenly bursts out.

We know Pansy has chain bound the guilt in her soul.

'Unchain it, Pansy, set it free. A lifetime of friendship, nothing to hide in the closet. It's a guilt we all share. And as the cliché goes, the truth will set you free.' And as an afterthought, Wan adds, 'Us too.'

'Ironically it's the guilt that's kept us together, it was a shared guilt,' I blurt out. 'Kim, Wan and I did talk about it, our summer place ghost.'

'Mary, we did only once, OK?' Kim snaps. 'We knew we had to talk about it, but we were afraid.'

'I egged Tony to do it,' says Pansy. 'It was more of a taunt. Did I really expect him to? I don't know. It was youthful exuberance, foolishness. Tony's parents called my parents when Tony did not come home that night. The next morning they called the police. A hotel staff had found a pair of sandals and a pile of clothes neatly folded under the angsana tree, had labelled them "Owner Unknown" and stored them in the storeroom. Tony's red car was in the car park. His blue naked body was fished out two days later, off a nearby island by fishermen. Alone, Tony had swum out to sea after the dance. Tony had confided in David, his brother that he thought it would be a great birthday present for me, to swim in our birthday suits, as I had suggested. But he wanted to test the sea first. David had encouraged him. Tony's parents said Tony had a fear of open water. He never told me. I then recalled that Tony never wanted to go swimming with me. He brushed me off with *"You want me to compare you with other girls in their bathing suits?"* I'm a strong swimmer. That Saturday night after we went home, Tony went back and did what he did.'

The police had been relentless, vindictive, and unforgiving in their interrogation. '*What alcohol, how much, what drug, how much, how much tobacco, how much sex? Orgy? Where?*' Alcohol, drugs, tobacco, sex, over and over. The drinks receipts saved us from the alcohol charge, but not the drugs, tobacco and sex. Our parents continued the interrogations. They forbade us to see one another, slapped on curfews until we matured into 'responsible adults'. The guilt followed us a long time. With time we had learned to 'let go', not to deny but to accept what had happened, not to blame anyone, but to be supportive of one another and move on.

Pansy had been devastated, had to be observed medically, and we suspected had not fully recovered from the ghost of the summer place past. Her parents decided it was best for her to work abroad together with a relative, no communication allowed. We lost Pansy for four decades.

'Pansy, Tony loved you very much, to do what he did,' Kim interrupts our thoughts.

'Tony, I did love him. I still do. Sometimes I doubted myself, did I love Tony? Or was it the guilt that convinced me I did?'

After the incident we were never the same. We lost our boys. But then again were they really ours? We three girls remained home, got careers, married and raised families. Kim later divorced,

Wan and I were widowed. We matured into senior citizens and doted on our grandchildren. In some unexplained way, Tony occasionally invited himself into our company.

'It wasn't your fault, Pansy. It was an unearned guilt, the worst kind of guilt to feel. It's a thief of time, love, truth,' Kim comforts her.

'Life isn't fair!' Pansy mumbles, bursting into tears. '*I'm gonna wash that man right outta my hair, I'm gonna wash that man right outta my hair, I'm gonna wash that man right outta my hair, and send him on his way.*'

Pansy confesses the reason she insisted we dine here. 'I've dreamt of Tony many times over the last year. It is always the same. There he is, always smiling his impish dimpled smile. We are on opposite sides of a gentle river. He blows me a kiss, waves and walks away. I throw one end of my scarf to him and he pulls it away. I run after him, but the river just gets wider and the water gushes. The wind whips up, and I can't reach him. Then I wake up. What does it all mean?'

'What do you feel when you wake up, Pansy?' we chorus.

Pansy is visibly agitated, her voice rising as she continues. 'Initially I cried, calling out to him. I thought he was inviting me to cross over to his side. I yearned for him, yet I was afraid. I wanted him to hold me in his arms, I wanted to feel sheltered, safe and secure. I wanted him to tell me he loved me, he had never said that. I didn't want to cross over to the other side. There was a great deal of inner noise, it exhausted me. It was pure selfishness to ask Tony to swim naked in the sea. I wanted to test his love. Was it real love? Was it because we had been together since kiddy days, we naturally allowed ourselves to fall into that trap called childhood sweethearts and eventually marry? Was it because we had wealthy parents who were buddies and had encouraged the relationship? But after several similar dreams, I knew that was his way to tell me to let go.'

I think aloud, 'Were our boyfriends really our boyfriends? Where are they now?'

A broad smile spreads across Pansy's face, 'I know what it means.'

'Pansy, that's wonderful.' Kim orders another round of drinks. We drink in silence. Silence is the great equaliser, each of us deep in our own thoughts.

Pansy calmly tells us, 'Since I went abroad I wore a neck scarf all the time. Melbourne is a windy city. And when I got home, I was never without it. Now I realize why I was never without a neck scarf. It was symbolic of being strangled. In my dream Tony pulls my scarf away, to set me free. So this evening, together we make it a shroud and sail it out at sea. It's Hermes, genuine.'

'Sure? Not from the back streets of Bangkok?' I say. 'Like the Vuitton bags you got us and convinced us into believing were genuine?'

'Mary, stop it!' Wan barks.

Somehow it is difficult to 'un-remember' Pansy's arrogance at us 'poor things' as she once described us to Tony. 'That's my necklace Mary is wearing. Gave it to her, poor thing.' I hated her then, do I still?

At the water's edge, Pansy's Hermes beige silk scarf with the little pink roses is tied up around handfuls of sand. We hold hands and set it free until it finds its home in the depths of the sea.

Pansy suggests, 'Let's drink some more. No one to return to, right? We live alone, so we better learn to like ourselves and do whatever we want. Life is short!'

'Life is short, don't make it shorter! Pansy, you're still the wild one! But then again, past our seventies, why not!' Wan giggles. We giggle a lot, the drinks have seeped into the giggling part of our brains.

'Yeahhhhhh. Let's drink to this 74-year-old virgin! We were young once and we were beautiful.' I look at Pansy, suddenly I no longer resent her making me wear that ugly yellow dress with red polka dots. I feel sad for her. She is so alone.

'Now we have mellowed, we are comfortable,' Kim adds, 'comfortable in our skin, not bothered our clothes have shrunk, men no longer on our menu, etc, etc. Notice, no wedding rings on anyone.'

We call for more drinks. The aroma of gin, vodka, rum, red wine, white wine and whatever else permeates the air. I'm not sure we are drinking to celebrate Pansy's 'liberation' or for no apparent reason, or we just don't know what else to do. I feel a strange queasiness but I cannot tell what it is. We listen to the soft music oozing from the clandestine speakers, 'Are You Lonesome Tonight?' It is past the Cinderella hour. 'Are You Lonesome Tonight?' Pansy asks, chin on one hand, the other hand clutching an empty glass, eyes beady, eye makeup smudged.

Pansy is in a singing mood, 'A song is not a song till we sing it. Let's sing it!' So we do, softly initially to get the right key and once found, we surprise ourselves that we can remember most of the lyrics. We sing the songs we used to dance to, at times off-key; when we forget the lyrics, we make up our own, each one different and we giggle. The singing envelopes us. What we have been unable to express in words, we sing: 'A Summer Place', 'Walk On By', 'Smoke Gets in Your Eyes', 'It's Only Make Believe', 'Heartaches by the Numbers' and many others.

This evening is the first time we have returned to the dance floor by the sea as a foursome since that fateful evening so long ago. We are a little drunk, but who cares? Finally, it is time to sing our Cinderella song, '*Good night Irene, Irene good night, I'll see you in my dreams.*'

To Zoom And Back

During the COVID-19 pandemic, there was a complete lockdown in Singapore. Grandma is an active member with the Seniors Group. They have their weekly activities, but with lockdown, they had only WhatsApp Chats. They then decided to learn how to Zoom, to chat online and 'see' one another. It was a learning experience, a curveball thrown to them. Nevertheless, the need to connect motivated them to learn Zoom. This is in large part their story.

Link: https://zoom/09876543/sayangme
Password: Sayangyou23

Grandma is glued to her new iPad. 'No, can't show you what I'm texting! Private, OK!' then she smiles her sweetest smile, eyes glitter, waves me away.

I live with grandma as my school is a ten-minutes walk away but I am soon to start undergraduate studies at the National University of Singapore. It feels suspicious to me that Grandma has not been glued to her Korean dramas every afternoon for the last week. When I come in, she hides her iPad under her blouse. I worry but she refuses to tell me or my parents anything. Dad asks me to probe, I'm her favourite grandchild. No, grandma's not telling, she looks fine and is more cheerful, humming and smiling, her fingers tap, tap, tap, her steps light.

One day she says, 'Hwee Lin, when you go to Uni next month, I can still chat with you and see you and see your room.'

'Of course, Grandma, WhatsApp is easy. Come visit.'

'Not moving an inch from my chair. I Zoom you!' So, that's what she has been up to, learning Zoom online. She has signed up to learn Zoom – introductory and refresher courses. Now she's ready to Zoom me, her children and friends. Several of her friends are not into Zoom yet – 'So difficult to login', 'No iPad', 'No computer', 'So old already, Zoom what?', 'WhatsApp can already', 'Meet and talk, much better'.

Grandma is not disheartened. She learns. She shares. And that's wonderful.

And this is grandma's Zoom life. She has mastered WhatsApp, as have her friends. But to them, nothing like their daily morning routines. Monday mornings band resistance exercise then to Kopitiam for breakfast and at times continue to lunch. Tuesday mornings she volunteers at the Seniors Centre. There she talks to the participants, plays gin rummy. Wednesdays are her visits to our Community Club to play *mahjong*. Thursdays are 'sleep-in' mornings. Fridays are her *makan kecil* potluck lunches with her friends, a group of twelve, each taking a turn to host. Saturdays are house-cleaning mornings with me. Sundays are 'whatever I like to do'. Daily afternoons are stay home Korean dramas, Not

To Be Disturbed. But with COVID-19 rearing its head over us we are cautious. Then Zoom zooms in like Superman and everything is alive again.

* * *

Grandma is a leader of sorts, and has several WhatsApp groups with different sets of friends. Her busiest chat group is her *makan kecil* potluck lunch group, naming themselves MK12 Chat.

COVID-19 makes a gentle debutante entrance. Nothing much to worry about, we were told. Three months later she throws off her genteelness to parade her spectacular self, COVID-19, public enemy number one. Empty parks, lifeless malls, weeping transport personnel, hand-wringing hospitality staff, 'Work From Home' notices, as well as 'School From Home'.

Grandma's WhatsApp chats however are alive and are in a frenzy.

'Hwee Lin, can help me WhatsApp? My fingers are so tired.'

'Grandma, you're on WhatsApp since morning. Why the need to chat so much?'

'I have many friends. They want to chat with me and everyone.'

'I want to Zoom my MK12 Chat, but only three of us know how to Zoom. You help me, can?'

Thus I become Grandma's little helper.

* * *

Grandma's WhatsApp to MK12:

—We Zoom, then we can see and talk to everyone. I have scheduled a meeting for this Friday, at 8 pm. Zoom is easy. You must login to join Zoom. My Zoom address is https:// zoom/09876543/sayangme. Password: Sayangyou23. Click on https:// then Password. You will see four icons. Click on JOIN. Then you will see 'Please wait, the meeting host will let you in soon'. I'm the host and I will let you in. Then you will see on top, Unmute, Start Video, Share Screen, Participants and More and under it dots. On the left in red, Leave and below that 9 little squares Switch to Gallery View. On the main screen you will see me. It's easy to follow. Can login at 7.50 to chat. Please RSVP you will join.

* * *

Friday 7.15 Grandma's WhatsApp reminder to MK12 to Zoom at 7.50.

WhatsApp chat at 7.50, Grandma's pitched voice on the phone, 'Yoke Keng why are you still not on Zoom? I already sent to our chat we Zoom. Come in NOW! Everyone waiting for you. Now!'

Grandma's MK12 Zoom
Join join join join.

* * *

On WhatsApp:

—Mavis, where got? I click nothing.

—You click on https?

—I copy from phone to my grandson's laptop.

—Check you copied address correctly.

—Mavis, where did you learn Zoom? Easy to learn or not?

—Easy. After we Zoom a few times, all become expert.

—Sorry *lah*, Mavis, I copied wrongly. My grandson says better to Cut and Paste, no mistake.

—Sorry, my phone battery 6%. My boy plays games until I also forget to charge. 6% battery can Zoom?

—Charge it now and can Zoom.

—OK, ten of us. Hello everyone. Can hear me? Donald said he's having dinner at daughter's house. Yue Lee did not reply. You see 'Unmute' button? Unmute so all can hear all.

—How ah? There is a red line on 'Unmute'.

—Click on it. Done? Now no red line right? Do the same on Start Video, if you see red line, click so that everyone can see everybody.

—Oh, ok got it. Now I can hear and see everyone. Hello.

—Hello, hello, hello.

—Now click 'Participants', you see names of our group. Yue Lee and Donald are not there. No go to left side click on 'Switch to Gallery View'.

—Now we all on. Talk about what?

—Wow, hello everyone. My first Zoom. Interesting to see everyone. Just say whatever you want. Agnes you're in pyjamas, ready to sleep?

—This not pyjamas. My home clothes.

—Sajuta, I saw you in the train yesterday. You and your granddaughter. She's a big girl. What class is she in now?

—Final year primary school. This year change format in the graduating exam. The first batch is the guinea pig batch. Usually easier or harder. We went to buy masks, very few pieces left.

—How much a box now?

—$12, $8. You can also buy two pieces. You read that cloth masks are not good. But all the same lah.

—You remember when our children were young, they watched 'Sesame Street'. Then they showed a gallery of the characters, like in a concert hall, the *atas*[80] seats, three or four levels, each character at a balcony. Now I see us, we are also, like 'Sesame Street'. I like Miss Piggy and Kermit the Frog. I think they got married.

—That's not 'Sesame Street'. It's 'The Muppet Show'.

—*Someday we'll find it, the rainbow connection, The lovers, the dreamers and me la la la.*

—Fatimah you remember the song. Can sing the whole song?

—It's Kermit's song. Only he can sing it. But Fatimah you can sing also.

Fatimah sings. (Everyone claps)

—*Wah*[81], Fatimah you sing so well. Next time can Karaoke.

—Yes, good idea. Mavis, your CC[82] has Karaoke Room? Can

---

80 Up. Used in context it means expensive.
81 Wow.
82 Community Club.

book for us?

—Yes, what day?

—Weekday afternoon better, not many people around. How much?

—I don't know. I can check and WhatsApp.

—Also check what kind of songs. Got 'Rainbow Connection'? Then Fatimah can sing and we learn from her. Fatimah can?

—Sure can. But depends what day and time.

—My son when he was a boy likes Cookie Monster. He's so cute and funny when he mimicked Yummmmm and shoved all the cookies in his mouth.

—This is so fun. Mavis where did you learn how to use Zoom. I also want to learn and can Zoom my children. Must I pay? How much?

—Nothing to learn. After a few times you know how to Zoom.

—How to schedule meeting, get https and password?

—Go to your Community Club. There are many programmes for Seniors. Online.

—If I click on 'Leave' …

—Heh, Sin Wee, why you leave, come back, come back.

—She left already, how to come back?

—Mavis can invite her again.

—She can't hear us. Must WhatsApp her to 'Join' again.

—Never mind, it's already 10. Two hours go so fast.

—It's great fun. Mavis make it weekly, can? Same day same time.

—Yes, yes, yes.

—You learn how to Zoom and we take turns to 'Schedule a

214 YOU MIGHT WANT TO MARRY MY HUSBAND

Meeting', like our MK12. Next week I'll host again. Good night.

—Now how to get out?

—On the left you see 'LEAVE' click. Good night everyone.

* * *

—Grandma, I'm on Zoom introductory meeting now with my prof and classmates. So silence please, no Korean drama, ok? Thanks. My prof is recording us on video.

—Then I better put on clothes.

—Grandma everyone can hear you. Ahaaaaaaa. Class please ignore my grandma. She has her clothes on!

—Hello Aunty Grandma. Hwee Lin, show Video please.

—Why?

—To see you better.

—Actually what Lek means is, he wants to *see* your grandma!

—OK, Hwee Lin, I join your Zoom. I have my iPad. I know how to Zoom.

—Grandma, NO NO NO! Go away!

—Then I sit beside you. Save electricity, use one iPad, not two.

—Wah Aunty Grandma, you very on.

—Go away, Grandma.

—Then send me link. I won't sit beside you. I know this is your tutorial. I won't say anything, only listen.

—No, Grandma, please go away, please.

—I want to get to know your friends.

—Yes, yes, yes, Aunty Grandma. We also want to get to know

you. Hwee Lin says you are very beautiful.

—Yes, like a sixteen-year-old virgin, did she say that?

—Prof Rajan, please tell my grandma to go away.

—I think she's delightful. Wish my grandma is like her.

—Profffff, I'm out. (*leaves*) Grandma, see what you just did. Now no one in class knows me and it's all your fault.

—I love you, Hwee Lin.

* * *

Grandma's MK12 Zoom.

Join join join join.

—Hello everyone. Good, all of us here.

—Sorry everyone, last week I had to babysit my grandchildren. And so noisy I decided not to join.

—Hi, Donald here. Last week I was at my son-in-law's birthday dinner. Small celebration at home. Only five visitors allowed. His neighbour so *kaypoh*[83], stood at his door and pretended to greet us. My daughter says he's *kiasu*[84], so afraid and count visitors to all the units. He's retired.

—Mavis, so karaoke room at your CC? And how much per hour?

—Yes, there is, but not functioning yet. No equipment as the room is being refurbished, new carpet, sound-proof room, everything new. Management can't say when it's ready for booking.

---

83 Busybody.
84 Afraid of not keeping up with others.

—Fatimah can you sing a song? A song we all know and easy to sing.

—OK what about 'Doe Ray Me'? I start, Doe, a deer, a female deer, Ray, a drop of golden sun, (*Others join in the singing*). One more time with feelings.

—Why need karaoke room? We karaoke Zoom, more fun. Free. No need to travel, no need to dress properly, make-up.

—Ya, but we don't know the words. I suggest, everyone choose a song, easy to sing song.

—Good idea. And we WhatsApp the words.

—But we don't know the melody.

—No problem. Google for the song you want. And you watch video get the melody and get the words. WhatsApp us the link.

—YouTube also can. When I was growing up, we wrote words of songs in our 555-exercise book, remember? Then we taught each other to sing. Now new technology.

—Ha, Sing Pau, you clever, know this. Where did you learn this?

—My grandson taught me. He's always listening to K-Pop. So loud and noisy, told him to use headphones. He says K-Pop must be loud, then only *shiok*[85]. I go deaf.

—Same here. I told my grandchildren during grandma's time we sang songs. Beautiful melodies with meaningful lyrics. Now you make noise and call it songs. Dance like monkeys, jump here, jump there, some no shirts on. They said, grandma you old school!

—All agree then. One song from everyone.

---

85 Great satisfying feeling.

—I share something with you, good news. I'm going to be a grandfather, third grandchild.

—Congrats, Wah Keow.

—Congrats. Girl or boy?

—Girl, due next month. All three grandchildren girls. All of them so pretty and cute. So *sayang* them, just love them. My daughter says I spoil them.

—Girl or boy all the same. Not like my parents and parents-in-law time, boy good. Girl a-l-s-o good *lah*. When I had my first child, Jessica you know her, right? You know what my mother told me, my mother, OK, she said 'Geok, you must get pregnant again fast, and give birth to a son'! *Alamak*[86], I was in labour six hours! And my Jessica was only five weeks old.

—What did your in-laws say?

—They said, 'Rest well. You are young, can have many children.' That means what? A son! How do I know I have boy or girl? Not like now, can scan and know girl or boy. So if girl how? So heartache for me.

—You have three boys and one girl. Everyone happy, ya.

—Same for us Indians. Boys good, girls OK only. My mother also said the same, have boys first, then you can have girls. How do I know boy or girl? So I told her, 'Mother if my first child is a girl, I give her away.'

—And what did she say?

—She slapped me, then she went to the temple, make offerings that I will have sons first, no daughters never mind. I have three sons, no girls.

---

86 My goodness.

—So your mum's prayers were answered.

—Times have changed. I believe MK12 does not think that way.

—No, no, never, no, we are the modern grandparents.

—It's already 10.25. Good night. Same day and time next week.

* * *

Grandma's MK12 Zoom.

Join join join join.

—Welcome everyone. Gallery view, please. Full house, great.

—Today is Hong Chan's birthday. She's 80. We sing Happy Birthday. One, two three. Happy Birthday Hong Chan, Happy Birthday Hong Chan, Happy Birthday Hong Chan, Happy Birthday Hong Chan.

—Thanks, dear friends. I'm so glad I have this group. My children sent me this message this morning '*Happy Birthday, Mum. COVID cannot have dinner, cannot visit to give you birthday gift*', that's all. 80 years should be grand birthday.

—Hong Chan, I tell you what. WhatsApp them that your friends are taking you out to lunch. Now Phase 2, eight can meet, we are twelve, so two groups of six. Also, they give you a nice present, you buy what you like, tell them how much and they reimburse you.

—OK. WhatsApp, I type for you. '*Dear David and Daisy, Mum's WhatsApp friends are celebrating my BD. 6 of us for lunch at Marriot Hotel and 6 for dinner at St Regis. 80 BD is grand celebration. They told me to buy something I like, and they together reimburse me. So don't worry that I'll will be alone on my 80 BD. Still love you and spouses and grandchildren lots.'* Everyone this sound OK?

—Now I post to you, you COPY and PASTE, and post to David and Daisy. Not FW, if FW then they know someone wrote for you.

—OK, today is our Karaoke session. I'll start. My favourite song to my girlfriend then, now my wife. 'I Want to Hold Your Hand' by the Beatles. That time, dating means her younger brother or cousin must go with us. No twosome. No holding hands. One, two, three …

—So, Kiang you sang that message to her, so romantic. I also chose a Beatles song: 'Here Comes the Sun'. I was practicing and my granddaughter asked me why did this group call themselves an insect? And who's her favourite artists? 'Michael Jackson' and 'Lady Gaga'.

—Michael Jackson died and buried. Pass.

—Ya, and that Lady Gaga, what lady. She earns so little, she can only afford quarter of a dress, at most half a dress!

—My song is Connie Francis 'Among My Souvenirs'. Long story short. I thought he liked me cos he gave me a red pencil box and a red pencil inside. Then he went to uni in Australia and that's the end. Dead or alive, don't know. I still have that pencil box and the pencil, so *sayang*[87], I didn't want to use them.

—Wow, from puppy love days to grandmother days. My song is 'Into Each Life Some Rain Must Fall' by the Ink Spots. I didn't do well to get into Uni, so went to Poly. I was disappointed

---

87 Love. In this contest, valuable, cherished.

and depressed. But my Dad, best dad in the world sang me this song and the two lines 'Into each life some rain must fall, but some day the sun will shine'. I went to Poly, graduated top student, got a scholarship to Uni to read Business Management. My dad was right, after the rain, comes the sun.

—Hello, hello, hello, David and Daisy replied. David says, '*Mum, Daisy and I have booked a table for dinner at the Ritz Carlton Saturday. I'll pick you at 6.30. Just nice 8 of us. And buy yourself anything you like, and Daisy and I will reimburse you.*' What do I say now?

—You bought a jade bangle, right? Take a picture and send. Type '*Yesterday I bought myself this jade bangle I always wanted. Your Dad promised me one, but we had to save for your education. Now he's no longer here. It's a beautiful green, purple and brown hues piece. It's $2260, after 15% discount cos COVID poor business. PayNow, PayLah, PayPal, PayCash, PayGiro to my account. Love you lots. See you Saturday.*'

—No lah, it's $1820.

—It's bangle AND *angpau*. Take. (*everyone agrees*). Our suggestion works.

—Every song has a meaningful story for us. Really enjoy this session so much.

—Same day, same time next week.

* * *

Grandma's MK12 Zoom.

Join join join join.

—Good evening everyone. Only Lucy not in.

—I was reading the news. COVID not going away any time soon. Maybe another circuit breaker. *Alamak*, *kena*[88] lock-in.

—We Zoom, no lock-in.

—Agree Lawrence, nothing like going out to *makan*, to enjoy a meal with good friends. Now no band exercise, no walks in the park. Zoom is reel life, not real life.

—Don't rush to buy toilet paper.

—Not we Singaporeans only. You read in Australia, in US, Malaysia, no toilet paper, masks, sanitisers.

—Karaoke lounge, a few cafes, restaurants were fined. No crowd control.

—They need the business. Can't blame them.

—Some young people were arrested by police for protesting in front of Ministry. They are supporting a student who claims she was discriminated against.

—If they had a Zoom protest, I'm sure no problem. Zoom protest, nothing damaged, no one hurt, all peaceful.

—Hey, Penny, how to Zoom protest?

—The judge or magistrate will hold a viral trial, remote control court.

—Then it will be settled out of court ya.

—Hey, that's funny.

—The US thing is big news. International news. Will our protesters get pressed up?

---

88 To get.

—We're not big news, we're not even little news. No, we will not get airtime on CNN, Fox, BBC, CNBC. On Channel 5, Channel 8 and CNA, yes.

—Lucy just join, welcome. You are in San Francisco? I see the bridge behind you.

—I changed my background.

—We can change our background? How?

—Mavis, you are in charge, did not teach us this.

—Better to see the real you at home. You can change to artificial background easy. Click 'More' you see background, choose what you like. Or you download photo you like and upload. Change as many times as you like.

—Ok we practice now.

There is lots of noise, questions, laughter, suggestions on backgrounds. It is great fun for MK12, they forget time. I whisper to Grandma, it's 11.35 pm.

* * *

Grandma locks herself in again, every morning.

'Grandma what are you doing, locked in your room every morning? What are you up to? What mischief?'

'My home, I can do what I like. I don't control you, you don't control me.'

So I let her be. She is up to mischief, the glitter in her eyes tells me so.

* * *

A week later.

'Hwee Lin, we are now into blogs. Blog login MS12. MS for Magnificent Seniors and we are 12.'

Grandma, that sounds like 'Ocean's 8', 'Ocean's Eleven', 'Ocean's Twelve', 'Ocean's Thirteen'.

'They are a gang of thieves. We are not. We are Magnificent Seniors 12.'

That's my grandma. Isn't she great?